from yesterday

by

Miriam Epstein

MIRIAM EPSTEIN

FROM YESTERDAY

by Miriam Epstein

Publication date: MARCH, 2014

First Edition

No part of this publication may be reproduced, distributed, or transmitted in any form or by any means, including photocopying, recording, or other electronic or mechanical methods, without the prior written permission of the publisher, except in the case of brief quotations embodied in critical reviews and certain other non-commercial uses permitted by copyright law.

The characters and events portrayed in this book are fictitious. Any similarity to real persons, living or dead, is coincidental and not intended by the author.

ISBN-13: 978-1497379466

ISBN-10: 1497379466

Copyright © 2014 Miriam Epstein

All rights reserved.

FROM YESTERDAY

chapter one

Sometimes I see my dead sister. I'm not seeing a ghost; I don't believe in supernatural phenomena or anything like that. It's just that once in a while someone will pass by me and I'll be reminded of Nicole because this person walks the way she did, or that person wears her hair in the same French braid that my sister used to favor. Then this person will turn around and the spell will break and I am left questioning my sanity. When this happens, I force myself to shake it off and realize that it couldn't possibly be her. I pray to whomever it is that people pray to, and I'm no longer sure that I believe in some kind of higher power, that this will be the last time it happens because it throws me off my game and I can't afford to let that happen.

So, of course, I see Nicole only moments before I'm walking into my Social Work with Diverse Populations course on day one of my Sophomore semester. This girl is wearing the exact same green Nike shirt with the purple swoosh splashed largely across the back that Nicole loved to wear to the gym. I take a step towards her, her name on the very tip of my tongue, and then she disappears as my vision is tarnished by utter and total blackness. Actually, it's the black t-shirt of the guy I just crashed into and I can practically taste the detergent he uses as my nose and mouth bounce off of the upper part of his ridiculously hard back. It hurts.

Annoyingly Buff Guy turns around and I can feel heat creep up the back of my neck to my ears in a haze of total humiliation, which almost counteracts the pain of walking into a mack truck with my face. His light blue eyes hold a healthy amount of concern in them and I immediately remember who I am and that the last thing I need is for someone to have any kind of concern for my well-being. I shove him out of my way, which isn't very effective because he's built like a linebacker, and step around him while giving him the evil eye.

Whatever words of concern he had prepared for me take a nosedive as I see his mouth drop open with incredulity. He recovers quickly because I hear his voice at my back only a second later.

"But *you* ran into *me*..."

I don't stay to listen to the rest, opting to find the emptiest section of the massive classroom and settle myself in a seat off to the side and towards the rear. I'm mentally patting myself on the back from having narrowly avoided talking to someone, which I try not to do, when the professor calls the class to order and begins to cover the syllabus. This is boring, as most of day one courses are because I can read the syllabus on my own as it is sitting right in front of me. Dr. Reyes has just moved on to the section in which he describes how our grades will be assessed when I hear a low voice come from behind me.

"That was kind of a bitch move."

I don't need to turn around to know who the speaker is, and tempting as it may be to tell him exactly where he can go, I remain facing forward and pretend I'm still listening to the professor. Then there is a scuffling noise from behind me and the next thing I know, Annoyingly Buff Guy is sitting next to me.

"Are you really going to ignore me?"

I really am. Hopefully my body language conveys this properly.

"I thought college girls were mature."

I will myself not to fall prey to his goading. My temper has become shorter with every moment I spend in Miami; a city full of people that lack the very basic manners one should possess in order to get through a day without being a total asshole. That's why I chose it.

"Come on, you ran into me pretty hard. It must have hurt. I just want to see if you're okay."

Clearly, he's not from around here. Which is evident by the very subtle undertone of Bostonian accent I can pick out of his pleas for my attention. Out of the corner of my eye, I see him inching closer to me and I sigh internally. He isn't going to give up any time soon.

I look down at my notebook and open it. Maybe if I pretend to take notes he will leave me alone. Or at least think I'm a complete nerd for taking notes on office hours. I'm doing such a good job of tuning him out that I don't realize, until it is too late, that Dr. Reyes has just assigned a project and dismissed the class. Fantastic. I have no idea what I missed and I will be forced to ask the professor and risk his dislike because he'll know I wasn't listening.

Before I can do that, though, Annoying and Ripped saves me the trouble because he obviously was paying attention all the while badgering me. I'm not sure what is worse; pissing off my professor or giving my new classmate the satisfaction of knowing he's just won this round when I'm forced to acknowledge him.

"Do you know what topic you'd like to choose?"

I stare at Ripped with what I'm sure is a dumbfounded expression on my face.

"You were ignoring me so hard that you completely missed the research project he assigned that is worth a huge percentage of our final grade. On the back of the syllabus is the list of acceptable topics. We have to choose one and email the professor with our decision by next class."

"We?" I ask.

FROM YESTERDAY

A smug smile lights his face right up. "Yes, we. Because you and I were the only students sitting on this side of the room, and partners were required to be chosen right away, you and I are working on this together."

I shake my head. "No. Absolutely not. I'll speak to Dr. Reyes. I don't do group work, and if I did, it wouldn't be with you."

And even more maddeningly arrogant now as he points out, "This is a required course to get into the Social Work degree program. Group and partner work is required for everyone. Even you. So, I don't think that will work out for you."

He's right and we both know it. "Fine," I grumble, and I walk quickly out of the classroom and into the hallway.

I'm almost exiting the building when he catches up to me.

"You walk fast."

Because responding with a "*Gee, Captain Obvious,*" type line seems a bit over the top, I let that one go..

"Look, I can tell you don't want to, but I'm going to need you to at least pretend to be a civilized person and tell me your name and give me your contact info. Forty percent of our grade, remember?"

I stop walking and face him. "My name is Paige. I'm not interested in being friends with anyone, not just you, so don't take it personally."

He opens his mouth to respond, but I stop him by snatching his notebook out of his hands. I write my name and number and my email address on the first page and hand it back to him before I walk away.

"My name is Brady," he says to my back.

I shrug my shoulders as if his name is completely unimportant to me, but the truth is, I'm intrigued. For the first time in over a year, I have managed to make a connection with someone. It should scare me, but it doesn't.

Chapter Two

South Florida University is located in a thriving suburb of Miami; more specifically the North Miami Beach area. The campus is set way back off of Federal Highway/US-1. There is a nice part of town right smack on top of a bad part of town and the school is a tiny bit closer to the not-walking-alone-at-night variety. Which is why I can't figure out who thought it would be a good idea to build a luxury high-rise complex in front of the school, just before the major road. Not many college students are walking around with the kind of finances that would afford them to live there.

I am not most college students. My father created a successful web based business during the era where large companies bought anything and everything having to do with thriving internet based small businesses. He sold his web domain just before that flame burnt out and made a sum of seven figures that he wisely invested. To say that my sister and I grew up spoiled would be an understatement. Both of our parents had careers they loved and took up all of their time. In lieu of their presence, we got anything we wanted and a Russian nanny that we adored. Malvina was with me and Nicole until I turned 14. Nicole was 17 and neither of us needed a caregiver, though you can be sure it was a sad day for all of us when she left. I saw her once more at the funeral.

When Nicole died, my grieving father combined our trust funds and gave everything to me. I didn't want the money my sister was meant to have and I still don't, but I can't deny that I grew up a certain way and campus dorms probably were not going to work for me. I like having my own bedroom and bathroom. When I moved here, I knew this building would be perfect for me.

It is less than a mile from campus to my apartment so I walk almost every day. August in Florida is incredibly humid and by the time I get home from my last class, I feel sticky and gross. Not even the frigid blast of air conditioning that hits me after I use my electronic key card to access the building is enough to keep from wanting to shower right away. I have to check my mail first, so I walk into the alcove behind the security desk that houses the postal boxes.

"This is ridiculous! Check your book again because you've obviously missed something."

The outburst of a disgruntled visitor is amplified where I am standing and I'm so startled that I drop my mail and my books on the floor.

"I'm sorry, sir, but I do not have you listed as a pre-approved guest. Until I have written authorization from the unit owner, I cannot let you in."

This back and forth continues between the guard and the visitor as I get on the elevator. It is true that the security in this building is pretty insane; you have to pass through three checkpoints, show your picture I.D., and wait for a phone call to the unit before you're allowed past the front desk. It drives people crazy and this is not the first time I've heard the poor front desk guy be yelled at. I love the tight security. It makes me feel a little bit safer to know that it's nearly impossible to get in here if you're not wanted, though I doubt that I will ever feel completely secure anywhere.

The ride to the twenty-third floor is quick and I'm through my door and in the living room in a matter of minutes. I set my books and the mail on top of the coffee table and sit down on my couch. Late afternoon light filters through the heavy curtains that I rarely open. Though I have lived here for a little over a year, I didn't bother with decorations. There is utilitarian furniture in every room; necessary pieces like a bed, dressers, tables all done in some kind of dark wood. There are no pictures, posters, or cutesy items that suggest someone lives here. I like things clean and uncluttered.

I have reading to do, a ton of it thanks to the over-eager professors in the School of Social Work, but I choose to close my eyes instead of cracking a book and I'm out in minutes.

Looking at Nicole is almost like looking into a mirror. Despite the three year age difference, my sister and I share the same Russian features, long brown hair, and hazel eyes. I haven't quite filled out like she has, though, and my fourteen year old body doesn't have the assets for the low cut mini-dress I just took out of her closet.

"Not that one, Rebecca. Try the green sweater with your black leggings. Green looks pretty with your eyes."

I run into my room and grab my leggings from the back of the desk chair. Malvina, our caretaker, left for an extended vacation last month and neither my sister nor I have spent a great deal of time putting our laundry away. It was hard enough to learn how to use the washing machine in the first place; we haven't gotten around to the actual folding and putting away so most of our clothes are in piles on the dresser or chairs.

"Like this?," I ask her as I re-enter her bedroom.

Nicole pauses from applying mascara in her vanity mirror and turns to look at me. "Perfect. Mascara and lip gloss and you'll be ready to put all the other ninth-graders to shame. Are you excited for your first high school dance?"

"I guess. I just wish I wasn't going alone. I don't really know anyone in my class yet."

"You're not going alone. You're going with me. All of my friends love you, so you already have people you can hang out with. And you'll make friends once you get there. That's the point."

I'm still a little uncertain, but I smile at my sister and try to shift the focus off of me and onto her. "Your dress is pretty, Nicole."

She looks down and tugs on the hem of her skirt. "You don't think it's too short, do you?"

It is and we both know it, but I shake my head. "No, it's perfect.

FROM YESTERDAY

And it's bright red so there is no way Jake won't notice you."

"Jake is a loser. I'm over him." *She lifts her favorite lipstick, MAC Russian Red, and paints the crimson on her lips. She always wears that color as either a nod to or in spite of our heritage, but tells me I'm too young for red.* "Can you keep a secret, Rebecca?"

"You know I will never share your secrets with anyone."

She pulls me into the hallway and grabs her purse off the doorknob. "I met this guy. He's a tiny bit older, but he's kind of incredible. I want you to meet him, so we're going to stop by his place on the way to the dance, okay?"

I'm uneasy. I barely want to go to this dance, let alone some strange guy's house. "How old is he?" *I ask.*

My sister frowns. "He's twenty-two."

"Five years older than you!"

She puts her finger to her lips. "Shhh. Lower your voice. Mom is home. It is not that big of a deal, Rebecca. Now grab your bag so we can go before--"

"Where are you girls going?"

The heavy Russian accent of my mother freezes my blood as it travels through my veins like ice water. She is almost never around, but on the few occasions we do see her, she has an unlikely ability to make us obey despite her lack of true parenting over the years.

Nicole steps in front of our mother and kisses her cheek. Being affectionate is not the strong suit of anyone in this family, but this move always seems to work for my sister. "We're going to the *dance, Mama. Remember? I told you all about it. Rebecca needs to make friends now that she isn't home schooled anymore."*

My mother nods. "I still don't understand why you want to go to a public school, either of you, but okay. You make sure to watch for your sister, Nicole. Home by eleven, yes?"

"Yes, Mama," we reply in unison.

But when eleven o' clock comes, neither Nicole nor myself are at home.

I wake up on the couch, drenched in a mixture of perspiration and despair. I remember every single detail of that night with shocking clarity for a five year relay. It was the last time I ever felt normal in my house.

The hallway leading towards my bedroom seems endless as I'm jonesing for a shower to wash away the grime and possibly the memory. I should go to the gym. An hour of cardio or a kick boxing class is always a great distraction and in Miami there is a gym on every street. I'm tired, though. The nap I took wasn't refreshing and I feel more out of it than I did before. Maybe even a little on the dizzy side. I'll look for something to eat once I'm clean.

I reach my bedroom and strip as I walk through to the bathroom, dropping each item of clothing on the floor and leaving it there. I don't do things like that anymore; I always clean up after myself, but I'm making an exception this one time.

It is dark in the bathroom and I have to feel around for the light switch. I find it and flip the lights on. I begin to scream, but eventually I lose the ability to make a sound so the screams choke the breath from my throat. I'm reminded of the time my sister and I learned how to make one another faint by cutting off our air supply for a moment. We called it California Dreaming. Only I don't just lose consciousness for a moment, I pass out.

When I come to, it is still there. I'm not hallucinating. On the counter is one of my many tubes of MAC Russian Red with the lid off. On the mirror, written in lipstick, is my sister's name.

chapter Three

Somewhere in my head I am able to acknowledge the wrongness of me standing in front of a mirror with a bright red NICOLE lipsticked over it and brushing my hair that is wet from a shower. It doesn't stop me from doing so. I yank the comb through my chin-length hair repeatedly and with force, ignoring the angry throb of the gash over my right eyebrow. I must have hit my forehead on the counter when I went down. Perfect. That will go really well with the scar on the same side on my lower lip.

I place my comb on top of the sink and look in the top left drawer for a bandage. There is a box of them next to some antibiotic ointment. Setting my hands on top of the counter, I lean forward and stare at myself in a piece of the mirror that isn't marked up. The image that reflects back at me is eerily similar to the one I saw a few years ago, after that night. The only thing different is the length of my hair. I have spent a great deal of time trying to erase that girl from existence, but no matter how hard I try, the old me keeps finding her way back to trip me up.

Reality smacks me in the face as I stand here feeling sorry for myself. Between the long shower I took and the time I spent getting dressed, I have been all alone in an apartment that someone had to have broken into. I have to get out of here.

I hurry to finish dressing. Shorts and a bra might be acceptable in South Beach, but I'm not going to an overpriced night club that is half an hour away but takes almost double that in traffic. Plus, I'm not skanky so I'll wear a real top. Minimal make up; just some mascara and gloss over a touch of concealer for the lip scar. I don't need anyone thinking I'm some kind of battered woman and attracting unwanted attention. There is little I can do about the fresh cut above the eye, though, so the flesh-colored bandage will have to do.

Before I'm out the door, I grab a can of pepper spray and a switchblade to keep in my purse. Just in case.

I'm locking my door when I hear an unfamiliar voice from down the hall.

"Hi."

I tense up, even though the voice is female, and turn to look while keeping one hand on my pepper spray. A pretty redhead, mid to late 30s I'd guess, is standing in front of the apartment two doors down from mine. She's carrying several grocery bags. I relax. She looks non-threatening. Not like a person who just vandalized my bathroom and violated my space, but that doesn't make her a source of comfort either. I try to avoid friendly people. I don't need a friend. I smile at her and head for the elevator. Before I make it there, I hear the unmistakable sound of groceries hitting the floor, followed by a few choice expletives from the woman. I sigh. This is not my day.

"Let me help you," I tell her as I snatch a stray orange from the floor.

"Thank you. I shouldn't have tried to carry so much, but I just moved in and I didn't know if there was a cart or something downstairs."

"The valet has one. Next time, just let them help you out."

She nods. We finish gathering the stuff that fell on the floor and I place it in the bags that didn't rip as she unlocks her door. If her unit is the same layout as mine, the kitchen will be near the entrance off of the foyer. I can set her bags down quickly and leave.

"Please come in. I really appreciate your help."

I'm right about the layout of her place and I have the stuff on the breakfast bar in no time. Even though there are several boxes still unpacked in here, I can't help but notice that her place looks much more lived-in than mine. It's warm and inviting. "No problem."

She extends her hand to me. "I'm Elyse. Nice to meet you."

I shake her hand. "Paige."

FROM YESTERDAY

"Well, Paige. I'm about to start dinner for my fiance and myself. He should be home in an hour or so. Obviously I have plenty of food. Can I invite you to join us?"

"I wish I could, but I'm on my way to the library to meet a classmate," I lie.

Her face falls slightly. "That's too bad. We moved here only a few days ago from Indiana. My fiance got a great promotion,but it's so far from home. I don't know anyone. Maybe another time?"

I feel guilty. I know what it's like to be far away from everyone you love, even if it was by choice. I nod my head even though I doubt it will ever happen. "Definitely."

I'm really on a roll with this lying thing. Elyse follows me to the door and holds it open for me.

"It was nice meeting you, Paige. Knock on my door anytime."

"Likewise, Elyse."

That makes two people that I have spoken to in one day for something other than a necessity. If I wasn't still so shaken by the love note in my bathroom, I would almost feel human again.

I take the elevator to the third floor and head into the parking garage. Though I prefer to walk, this is Miami and public transportation is a joke here. I bought an Acura MDX when I moved here. It is the same car Nicole used to drive.

The Starbucks on Biscayne and 190th street is unusually quiet for a late afternoon, but I'm thrilled by this because I'll actually have a place to sit. I choose an overstuffed armchair near the restrooms. People don't like to sit close to bathrooms, but I don't care. I pull out my iPad and load the school's online course web page. I take as many courses on the web based service as possible because I'm self-motivated enough to get my work done without someone telling me to and I really enjoy sleeping late. I took an 8 am class the first semester of Freshman year and I got a C simply because I slept through it so many times my professor lowered my grade. Never again.

I'm taking one of those lame syllabus quizzes that you have to do just so your instructor knows you logged on, when I see a shadow fall across my lap.

A male voice. "Mind if I sit?"

Without bothering to look up I tell him, "Yes. I mind."

"Be careful, Paige. I might start to think you don't like me."

My head snaps up. Of course it's Brady that is standing over me. My day gets better and better. "I don't know you well enough to dislike you, Brady. I just really like to study alone."

He sits in the chair next to mine, regardless of my obvious discomfort. His position is legs open and he leans towards me with his elbows resting on his thighs, macho-style, yet there is a quiet grace in the way he carries himself. It does not go unnoticed. I think that if I had not allowed myself to become an embittered version of me that I would like him. I can respect a person that will take my insufferable attitude and not only brush it off, but volley it right back at me in a manner that both disarms and excites. Also, he is damned attractive. Dark blond hair and blue eyes are a deadly combination. "I'm willing to bet that, if you give it some time, you'll take at least three or four weeks before you decide to dislike me."

There is undisguised mischief in his voice. If I didn't know better, I might think he is flirting with me.

Except I don't know any better. I prove this by standing up so quickly that my knees smack into the end table where my coffee is resting. Was resting. One second the cup is upright and the next it is not. I watch the still hot liquid cascade over the side of the table and deposit itself directly in the lap of one annoying and extremely good looking male.

Embarrassment fights its way to the surface but I stuff it back down. Show no weakness.

Brady is quite good at hiding his own feelings, because that could not have felt good. Yet he says nothing. Nothing turns quickly into disbelief as I snatch my things and force a smirk onto my lips.

"You're just going to leave me like this?" he asks.

"Of course not," I tell him. "I'm not a total bitch."

I toss a few napkins in his direction and I'm gone before

MIRIAM EPSTEIN

he can see my face turn red.

Chapter Four

I only have classes on Monday, Wednesday, and Friday so I don't have to see Brady today. I'm definitely feeling a lot of guilt over the way I've treated him when it seems like he is just a nice person. It just isn't a good idea for me to have people try and get to know me. It's bad enough that Elyse was in the building gym the same time that I was this afternoon. She came right over to the elliptical next to mine and struck up a conversation with me. She didn't seem to care that I had headphones on and was listening to music, she pantomimed for me to remove them. Reluctantly, I turn Thirty Seconds to Mars off and place the ear buds in the cup holder.

"Hi, Paige. I told Garrett, that's my fiance, all about meeting you yesterday. He wanted me to thank you for helping me with the groceries and invite you to dinner next Tuesday night. He left this morning to fly back home and finish up one last client account. He'll be home Monday night. What is your favorite food? I'll make it."

Ambushed. I felt completely ambushed by this ball of

energy of a woman. That, coupled with the fact that I couldn't think of a good enough excuse for a week from now must be why I tell her I'll come to dinner. "Okay, I'll be there."

Elyse increases her stride on the elliptical. "Fantastic! What would you like me to make? Are you allergic to anything?"

"I'm not picky. I'll be fine with whatever you make. I don't have any food allergies that I know of."

"I'll think of something. I can't wait for you to meet Garrett. Sorry to interrupt your workout."

I start to put my ear buds back in. "No problem. I've still got a while to go."

She opens a magazine. I have no idea how anyone can read while they are gliding back and forth on a cardio machine, but I'm certainly jealous because I wish I could make the time pass faster that way. Instead, I close my eyes and lose myself to Jared Leto singing about punishment, pleasure, and pain.

The truth is, I like Elyse. She has an easy-going nature about her that brings a semblance of calm to my inner nut job. For one moment, yesterday, I felt like I was visiting a friend when I was at her place. Eerie. I deny and deny and deny every chance I get to make a meaningful connection to someone and I know it's because of her. I died right along with Nicole that night and everyone knows it. My parents knew; that's why they sent me away that time. It's why I ran

FROM YESTERDAY

as far away as I could and didn't tell anyone how to find me. I just wish I could find myself.

chapter five

I'm early to class. Very early. I couldn't sleep at all knowing I was going to have to face up to my childish behavior in the coffee shop the other day, so I hit the gym before class and now I have the nervous energy of a woman going on a blind date. Maybe Brady will be late and I won't have to talk to him. Won't have to apologize, or look into those blue eyes and try hard not to revert back to the shy little mess of a kid that lost her voice when boys came around. Boys grow up and girls become women, but I haven't changed much.

Shut up, I tell myself. If I spent a little less time being melancholy and more time focusing on my school work, I'd probably graduate early. And when did I get so down on myself anyway? I spent precious time learning the fine art of I Just Don't Give a Fuck for a damn good reason. Nicole would be disappointed.

The new boyfriend lives in a small apartment complex made up of a U-shaped two story building centered around a massive swimming pool. Because temperatures have already been dipping into the low 60s and sometimes 50s, this and most pools in the area have already been drained.

Nicole parks her SUV in a guest spot. I don't bother to take off my seatbelt and get out.

"Come on, Rebecca. Let's go up."

I pick at an imaginary piece of lint on my skirt. I don't want to get out of the car. We shouldn't have come here. This is about twenty minutes outside of our neighborhood and it's not the safest area. "Can't I just wait here while you say hello or whatever? I'm sure this guy would rather see you alone, anyway."

Nicole unclasps my seatbelt. "No, Rebecca. Turner really wants to meet you. I've told him all about you and he's excited to meet my adorable little sister. Besides, it's cold and I don't want you down here all alone. I promise this will be quick."

I acquiesce as I always do when it comes to Nicole. We make our way past the lifeless swimming pool and up the stairs of the deepest set part of the building. All the doors are painted dark red and set just a bit farther back from the brick facade of the walls. Turner lives dead center of the second floor. He must have been watching for my sister because he opens the door before she can knock.

"Hi there, gorgeous. You look stunning."

Tall, sandy blond hair, and eyes that could be blue or gray depending on the light, it is easy to see why my sister is infatuated with him. And she is, I can see that clearly by the way her eyes light up as he pulls her in for a hug and spins her around. It's a rare *thing to excite her. He has charisma.*

Setting her back to her feet, Turner swivels in my direction and offers me his hand. I move closer for the handshake, but he grasps my hand in his and brings it to his lips. "And you're the lovely little sister. That gene pool of your family is quite impressive."

Ugh. My teeth ache from the sickly sweetness that drips from his corny sentiments. Nicole, never the one to hold back no matter how in lust she may be, swats his behind and moves past him into the apartment. "So, cheesy, Turner. Dial it down a notch."

He laughs and lets go of my hand only to take my arm and pull me inside. I squirm out of his hold as subtly as I can, but I don't want him to touch me. He has all the charm of a rattlesnake. Other than his ridiculous greeting, I have no reason not to like this man, but I don't. I can't say I'm the best judge of character; I'm pretty sheltered, but my guard is up. Maybe it's the age difference? I know I'm fourteen and I should be all excited and giggly that my sister met an older guy because sisters are supposed to be supportive, but I'm grossed out by it instead. I remember reading a book about a serial killer named Ted Bundy. This guy was good-looking and charming, which made him seem unassuming to women he would meet. Then he'd coax them into a more private setting where he proceeded to rape and kill them. A sociopath.

Turner reminds me of Ted Bundy.

"Come sit down, Rebecca. Make yourself at home."

I shake myself out of my dark reverie and join my sister and Turner. I know I have an overactive imagination. I'm probably just nervous about the school dance and I'm making everything into a

FROM YESTERDAY

bigger deal than it is.

"Hello, Paige."

Damn. I must have spaced out for a while because the lecture hall is full now and Brady is in his seat, next to me. His hair is slightly askew, as if blown by a sharp gust of wind. He really is striking.

I nod. "Brady."

"Spilled any good hot beverages lately?"

Okay, admittedly I should have apologized first thing, but the infuriating smirk on his face is making me want to slap him. Or maybe kiss him. Not sure.

No, that's not true. I am sure. I am sure that even if I want to kiss him, I won't.

"Look, Brady, I'm really sorry about that. I didn't do it on purpose, I promise. I was in need of a little alone time and you being there was a bit much for me."

"I appreciate your apology, Paige, but if you really wanted to be alone, why didn't you stay home? Public places don't exactly scream solitary confinement."

"Shhh. Class is starting."

I turn my head in the direction of Dr. Reyes, who is in fact standing at the lectern; notes in hand. I feel, rather than hear, Brady sigh in frustration and I know I've made my point. Hopefully he will give up trying to be nice to me from now on. Then I can feel like less of a bitch when I blow him off for this project and do the work for both us. He can put his name on it if he wants, or do his own thing. I can't afford to care. I try to block Brady from my thoughts and listen as Dr. Reyes talks about the group project.

"Keep in mind, students, that how well you work with your partner is going to be worth fifty percent of the assessment. I'll be asking both of you to fill out a rubric designed to answer my questions about that. Remember, this is a course for a major in Social Work. You will need to have the skill necessary to work with people. This won't be a project that one of you completes on your own and then calls it partner work. I'm sorry, Type A's, you're going to have to let go."

It's like I'm cursed. A condescending half smile is worn by Brady for the rest of the class.

FROM YESTERDAY

chapter six

"Miss Kerimov? Excuse me, Miss Kerimov?"

The front desk supervisor in my lobby has to call my name twice before I realize he's talking to me. A year and half and I'm still not used to that. I turn around to face him. His name tag tells me his name is Victor. Victor looks like he is in his forties and has the face of someone who takes his job seriously.

"Please, call me Paige."

Victor bends down and lifts the package up on the desk. "This came for you earlier by a private courier. It didn't require a signature so we allowed them to leave it here."

The box is wrapped in brown parcel paper and it is fairly large. Like, the kind of large that could fit a human head inside of it. Yes, I could stand to be a bit less morbid. I pick it up and shake it. The box is very light and makes only a slight rustling sound. Convinced that it is not a bomb, I decide to bring it upstairs.

"Thank you, Victor. Have a nice evening."

He smiles. "You do the same, Paige."

The elevator ride is soothing. I like white noise; almost any form of it can calm my nerves. I'm still feeling unsettled from my discussion with Brady in class. Or maybe it is just Brady himself that has me rattled. He's so frustrating, yet equally patient and kind. I noticed earlier that just having him sit next to me in class is kind of nice. This is not good. I do not have a crush on this guy.

My apartment is hot. No, it's beyond hot. I must have turned off the A/C when I left this morning. I chuck my bag and the package on the kitchen counter and go to the thermostat. It is set to its usual seventy three degrees. Fabulous, the thing must be broken. I'll probably die of heat stroke up here. I place a quick call to maintenance. They tell me they will have it fixed by eight o' clock this evening. Okay, do I spend the next three and a half hours sweltering in this hot box or should I take off? I could go to the gym, but then I'd have to come back up here and shower which will leave me sweaty even after the rinse off.

I could use the gym on campus. It's pretty nice and it has locker rooms with clean showers. Maybe I'll grab dinner on the way back. I pack some soap and shampoo in my gym bag. I find an old pair of flip flops that I don't mind getting wet; the locker rooms might be clean but I'll never put my bare feet on a public floor like that, and I'm good to go. I throw the package in my gym bag on the way out the door. I can open it later.

I run into no one on my way downstairs and the walk back to campus is equally uneventful. I get to the gym and quickly change in the locker room. There is a Spinning class starting in forty-five minutes that I'd like to try. I sign my name on the sheet posted to reserve a bike. I can kill time by doing some ab work, so I head over to the mats and turn my mp3 player on so that Florence and the Machine can motivate me.

I'm listening to Florence belt out Blinding, one of my favorite songs, when I feel someone tap my leg as I'm finishing up my last Turkish get up. I open my eyes and damn it! This guy is everywhere. I flinch when I realize his hand is still touching my leg. He pulls it away quickly.

"I'm sorry, Paige. I didn't mean to scare you. I just wanted to say hello, but you had your eyes closed and your music on."

He looks genuinely sorry and I feel like a jerk yet again. "No, I'm sorry, Brady. You just surprised me."

He smiles the first non-condescending smile I've ever seen on his face and I die a little. He crouches down to the floor so that we are a bit closer to eye level. "Are you just getting here, or is abdominal torture in the form of get ups the end of your workout? Nice form, by the way."

I laugh and pretend I don't notice the not so subtle wink he gave me at the end of that sentence. "I just started. I was doing abs to kill time before the Spinning class."

Brady smirks. "Spinning, huh? This I want to see."

Ugh. He had to ruin our nice conversation. I jump up to a standing position and shove him. He stumbles face first into the mat I was just sweating on and the woman beside us cracks up. "Always a pleasure, Brady. Now go away."

He laughs. "Sure, Paige, I'll go away right now. I'm certain that I will be seeing you soon."

"Whatever you say."

Brady walks off and I turn my music back on. A few more sets of crunches and twists and I see it is almost time for the class. I make a quick dash to the juice bar to buy a bottle of water on my way. I'm pretty sure water and a towel are a requirement for cycling classes. And if they are not, well then they should be. I know I will manage to sweat buckets during this type of class and I like to rehydrate and clean up after myself. One can only hope the other gym patrons will do the same.

The gym on campus is impressive enough to boast its own cycling room. The chain I usually work out in has you drag the bikes to the middle of the aerobics room for each class. I might be canceling my other membership soon. The room is dark, I'm pleased to see. This class should always be done in the dark. All the bikes are numbered and I don't have any trouble finding the one I signed my name next to on the sign up form. It has clip-less pedals. I'm psyched. I dig my mountain biking shoes out of my bag and change into them. They are lime green with hot pink accents and black laces. Ugly, as far as bike shoes go, but they reminded me of watermelons. When we were very little kids, Nicole and I used to save all the black seeds from the watermelons we ate and plant them in the backyard. She told me that we could grow a really big watermelon if we had enough seeds and I believed her. Eventually, she told me that we planted so many seeds that the melon would grow so big it would knock our house down. I cried hysterically, of course believing everything my big sister told me. She apologized for days afterward, having felt bad for upsetting me.

I miss those days. I miss my sister.

Shake it off, I tell myself. I adjust the bike to my hip height and handle bar preference and grab my towel. I'm settling myself on my bike when I hear an all too familiar voice come to life over the stereo, asking if anyone needs assistance getting set up.

You have got to be fucking kidding me.

Brady is standing at the front of the room next to the instructors bike, playing with his mic and the sound system. He looks up for a moment, catches my eye, and gives me the sexiest smile I have ever seen on a guy. I nearly fall off my bike.

Is the universe trying to tell me something? There has to be a reason why I run into Brady everywhere I go in the two or three days since I've met him. It's going to be really hard ignoring a really attractive guy that pops up all over and pays attention to me. At the very least, I need to focus on tuning him out during this class or I won't be able to truly enjoy it. Spinning is an experience; it's a mental toughness even more than a physical one to push yourself through some of those steep climbs. Do it enough and that toughness will insert itself into your every day life and help you cope with the difficulties. I know it did that for me.

The class begins and I'm immediately impressed with Brady's coaching style. He's a quiet motivator; there is no obnoxious yelling and he never touches the resistance on anyone's bike. He tells you how challenging the ride should be and then lets you make your own decision of how many times to turn the resistance dial. I like that type of instruction. His music is also good. Though I was a bit self-conscious at the start of the class, I quickly lose myself to the rhythm of my fly-wheel and I'm in my zone. His music is inspiring even; M83's Wait comes on during a particularly steep climb and it is exactly the right song to push me through.

All too soon, the class is over and I have to dismount the bike back into my slightly sad reality. I wipe the sweat off of my bike and drain my water bottle before I head to the locker room.

"Paige, hold on a second."

I pause at the exit of the Spinning room. Just outside the door sits a woman wearing a neon pink sequined sweat suit and it's seriously distracting. I turn around just as Brady is catching up to me and he has to put a hand on the wall behind me to keep from slamming into me like I did to him the first day of classes. Because he is leaning forward, our mouths are mere milimeters away from each others. I can practically taste his lips on my own. I could just lean towards him a little bit...

I realize what I'm doing before it is too late and I step under his arm and around him. "You should watch where you walk, Brady. You almost ran into me. I didn't know you were so clumsy."

To his credit, Brady deflects my obnoxiousness and even manages not to throw it right back in my face as I am really the clumsy person here.

"You did really well in the class. How long have you been taking cycling classes?"

"A few months. How long have you been teaching them?"

He thinks for a moment. "Officially, I've been a certified instructor since I was 18 years old."

I wait, but he doesn't elaborate. So I ask, "Unofficially? I'm sensing you are withholding information here."

He shrugs. "I could tell you, but you'd have to agree to come and have dinner with me first."

The thing is, I really, really want to. I'm dying to say yes. I just can't give in. So instead, I bristle. "I'm not going out on a date with you."

Brady looks almost contemplative for a moment before the self-satisfied smirk that he is so good at settles back over his face. "Aren't we presumptuous, Lovely Paige. I never said anything about a date. We both need to eat after that workout and it will give us a chance to talk for a while. Unless you have something better to do?"

He arches one eyebrow and looks at me pointedly, like he already knows the answer to that question is no. He's right; I have nothing better to do, nor is there anything I'd want to do more. Well...

Screw it. "I'd kind of rather watch paint dry, to be perfectly honest, but the air conditioning is being fixed in my apartment right now so let's go. I'm going to grab a shower first."

Brady laughs. "I'm glad I'm your first choice. I'm going to shower as well. Meet you in front in twenty minutes?"

"See you then."

chapter seven

Brady is leaning against the wall outside of the womens' locker room when I exit. He looks hot in jeans and a blue t-shirt that skims his muscular chest and arms and makes his blue eyes bluer. When he sees me, he lifts off of the wall and stalks over towards me; almost predatory in a way. The gaze he sweeps over my body makes me very glad that I threw skinny jeans into my bag, along with a very low cut black shirt. I was even lucky enough to have remembered my make up bag. Nicole always told me a woman should never go anywhere without first applying her mascara.

"Hi."

He takes my bag and slings it behind him. "Hi, yourself. You look great."

I try not to let him see how much I enjoy that comment and I start walking in the direction of the parking lot. After a long moment, I hear him sigh and he falls into step beside me.

"You're not going to make this any easier for me, are

you?"

I shake my head. "No, probably not."

Brady stops walking next to a black and red motorcycle. He pulls the strap of my bag over one shoulder and settles it across my body; I can see he is careful not touch me anywhere that might be inappropriate. Once my bag is in place, he looks up at me and brushes a strand of my hair behind my ear. Why is the simplest of gestures enough to makes ones knees shaky?

"That's okay, Paige. I respond very well to challenges."

And with that he leaves me practically breathless as he turns around and grabs a helmet from the back of the bike.

I finally find my voice. "What are you doing?"

He hands me the helmet. "I'm getting you set up. I'm sorry I don't have anywhere to store your bag, but it should be fine around you like that. Let's get this helmet on you, though."

I step back and refuse to take the helmet from him. "I'm not getting on that thing."

He looks confused. "Why not? You said you'd come out to dinner with me. It's perfectly safe."

"I... I don't think I can."

I will my voice to sound even and my hands to stop shaking. Brady's expression softens and he puts a big hand on my shoulder.

"You've never been on a bike, have you? I've had bikes

since I was fifteen and I'm very good. I promise to take it slow and get you there safely. Trust me, okay?"

Some part of me is screaming in my head, telling me this is a bad idea. I decide to throw caution to the wind and nod my head. If he would just take his hand off of my shoulder, I might be able to make better choices. It's too late now, though, and within five minutes I am wearing his helmet and he is helping me onto the motorcycle. He gets on in front of me and turns his head to look at me.

"Okay, just wrap your arms around my waist and press your body up as close to mine as you can."

The expression on my face must be very telling because now he's cracking up. "I'm kidding. You can just hold on to my hips if you want. If you're scared, though, you should wrap your arms around me, but you don't have to press your chest into my back."

I give him as dirty a look as I can, considering half of my face is obscured. "Jerk," I tell him, but I wrap my arms around his waist anyway and all of a sudden I love motorcycles.

The bike roars to life and Brady squeezes my right hand with his before grabbing the handlebars. And then we're moving. He is going slowly, like he said, but the feeling of the bike tilting slightly as we round the corners of the campus parking lot is a little bit scary. He keeps his word and doesn't drive like a maniac once we hit the nearly deserted service road that takes us from the campus to Biscayne Boulevard.

When we stop at the light, Brady puts one foot down and turns to look at me.

"Okay?" he yells over the roar of the engine.

I'm still clinging on to him for dear life so I simply nod my head. The light changes and we're moving again. I just close my eyes and try to ignore my fear of decorating the road with my body parts and just enjoy being able to be physically close to another human being without freaking. It is short lived, however, because not even five minutes pass by before I feel the bike slow down and pull into a parking lot. Reluctantly, I let go of Brady and work on getting off the bike without touching the exhaust pipe as he told me. I even manage to do it gracefully; I keep myself from falling headfirst onto the pavement.

"You like sushi?"

I look up and realize we are at one of my favorite restaurants in South Florida. It's one of those little Japanese/Thai combo places that looks like a dive, but has surprisingly great food. "I love this place."

"Perfect."

He holds a hand out towards me and I look at him, confused. Are we supposed to hold hands now? That wasn't part of the deal and it won't help me pretend I'm not attracted to him. After a moment, he reaches for the strap of my bag and I realize my mistake.

"Let me carry that for you," he says.

"Thank you, but I'm fine. You don't have to do that."

He gives me a look. "Paige, please allow me to be a gentleman and let me carry your gym bag for you."

I relent. The stern nature of his 'request' is actually really sexy. "Ok. Be thankful that I prefer black to pink or you'd look a little bit ridiculous right now."

He holds the door to the restaurant open for me. "I wouldn't mind carrying your pink bag around, Paige."

I roll my eyes as we walk up to the hostess stand, but before we can request a table, Brady snags my wrist and pulls me so that my back is leaning into his chest. I can tell he lowers his head down because next I feel his breath by my ear. "Roll your eyes at me again, Paige. I dare you."

He puts a hand on my hip and moves me forward, but I would have preferred to stay right where I was a second ago. The little power game he just played was inexplicably sexy. I can almost guarantee that if some other guy had just said that to me, while putting me in a physically inferior position, I would have punched him. Instead, I follow him to the little booth near the back of the restaurant that the hostess is taking us to. There are very few parties in the place, and our table is fairly secluded. I'm betting this is all a part of Brady's plan. Plan? What am I even thinking? There's no actual indication that he's interested in me for anything more than friendship and a great partner project. It's not unlike me to read into every little thing a person does and all the lust swirling around in my brain could very well be making me think this is more than it is. I have got to remember that or things could be very embarrassing for me. Again.

I will not let that happen.

Grabbing onto a semblance of the girl who doesn't let people in, I put up as much of a wall as I can before sitting across from Brady in the banquette. He makes eye contact and smiles at me, but I'm saved by the server who comes to hand us menus and I focus all my attention on ordering some water. Brady orders a Japanese beer and I risk a quick glance in his direction once the server walks away. He is frowning.

"Where did you go just now?"

I know what he's asking, but I play dumb. "What are you talking about?"

"It's like you just had a major mood swing or something. I thought we were making progress, you and I. You haven't even spilled anything on me today, yet. All of a sudden you seem like you're not in the same room with me anymore. Why do you do that?"

I shrug like I couldn't care less. It's an act, but I happen to be particularly good at this act. Usually. "Really, I have no idea what you mean. I'm here sitting right in front of you, Brady. Let's just drop it and order. I'm starving."

Just let it go, I will him. And he does, for a little while. We order our food and then spend a few minutes in what seems like companionable silence; each of us lost in thought.

FROM YESTERDAY

It doesn't last.

Brady places his arms on the table and laces his fingers together. "How many friends do you have, Paige?"

I am mid-sip of my water when he asks this and I nearly choke. "What kind of question is that, Brady?"

"A valid one. I'd like to know if this is about me or you."

"Well, you don't mince words, do you?"

He shakes his head. "No, and neither do you. Which is why I feel perfectly comfortable having an honest conversation with you. I'm not judging you or trying to be a jerk, I just really want to know if you'll ever open up a little more."

Something about the way he looks at me right then is my undoing. Immediately, I feel my defense mechanisms stripped away from me like a ribbon undone from a wrapped present. I can't do a thing to stop it. The somber mood lifts a little as I drop the straw wrapper I'm playing with and look directly at him. "I don't have any friends."

Something changes between us right then. It's like, with that one sad statement, I have finally let Brady in to my life. It is his first honest glimpse of who I am and he didn't have to pull it out of me forcefully. The words left my mouth willingly, knowing that I can no longer hide from him.

"Well it seems to me as if that is just a little bit untrue, Paige, because from where I sit it looks like the number of friends you have just increased by at least one."

I swallow hard. The lump in my throat is massive, but there is no way I will shed a tear. I've been vulnerable enough for one evening. Our server, bless her, arrives with our food and the semi-intimate moment Brady and I are sharing is drifting off with the aroma of ginger, garlic and cumin. I have never been so happy to see a plate of Pad Thai in my entire life. I grab my chop sticks and dig in while Brady does the same.

I think about Brady and Elyse and how these two people have managed to get more out of me in one week than any person has in years. Is there something different about either of them, or is it me who is changing? There was a time, most notably right after I left when I swore that I'd never trust a soul ever again. My sister had been the only one I had ever felt super close to; certainly not my parents then or now, and I didn't think I would ever need or want friends.

I suppose it is me that is evolving. It was inevitable, really.

One entire wall of the restaurant is a waterfall. I'm fixated by the water rushing down into the incredible jade and emerald stones that line the bottom. If this thing was in my apartment, I'd never leave it. I could sit and stare at it for hours.

"You gone for good there, Paige? Come back to me."

I look up into Brady's infectious grin and I feel a slight smile tug at the corner of my mouth. I must have been staring at that waterfall for longer than I thought because we've both managed to eat half of our plates even though it felt like only a minute had passed. "It's just that waterfall..."

"...is amazing," he finished for me. "I know. Mesmerizing. It's distracting both of us from talking, though, and I was really hoping to get a few complete sentences out of you tonight."

"Oh, stop. I've said plenty."

And then, in a move that just reeks of maturity, I stick my tongue out at him. He stares at me for a moment, seemingly stunned. I'm mortified. Why on earth did I just do that? My humiliation is short lived, much to my relief, because a second later Brady is laughing so hard I'm afraid he will choke.

"It's nice to see you enjoy yourself, Paige."

I look back down at my food and twirl my chopsticks around a few noodles, but I don't bother bringing them up to my mouth. He's right. I don't laugh anymore.

Needing to shift the attention away from myself, I change the subject. "Didn't you promise to tell me all about your sordid history of underage Spinning instructing?"

He nods. "I suppose I did say something like that, didn't I? It's not really all that interesting, much less sordid."

I pick up the bottle of soy sauce with the red cap and point it at him with the implied threat of flinging some at him. "I was joking. Now spill, before I do."

Brady reaches over and wraps one of his hands over top of mine, the one holding the sauce bottle. He doesn't remove it. "There is a very tasteless joke about being wet and salty somewhere in all of this, but I'm too much of a gentleman to make it."

I'm quite shocked and amused at what can only be seen as lewd innuendo and trying hard not to giggle all at once. He raises one eyebrow at me as if daring me not to give in.

"Anyway, the deal with the cycling is simple. My parents used to own a fitness center back home, in Boston. I practically grew up in that gym, and I loved to take the cycling classes when I was finally old enough to try. When I was sixteen, almost half of the staff had the flu at once and no one was able to teach the evening class. It was a really popular class and the members would have rioted if we had canceled it, so I filled in. That's it. Not a very interesting story, is it?"

His hand is warming my own and I'm lost in his words so it takes me a moment. "It is, actually. I like hearing about how people grow up. You sound like you really loved it there, so why did you come all the way to Miami for school?"

He smiles again, but this one doesn't reach his eyes. "My mother died of breast cancer a few years ago. Before that, there had been some amazing offers for my parents to sell the gym, but they never wanted to. When my mother passed, my dad sold the gym he had built with her and retired."

A single tear drop defies me and leaks out of my right eye, traveling a jagged path down my cheek. Brady takes his hand off of mine and wipes the tear away with one finger, then cups the side of my face and pulls me a little bit closer to him. "Don't be sad, Paige. I've grieved already. I will always miss her, but I have wonderful memories of my mother to take with me."

I close my eyes and lean into his hand without thinking. I'm sad for him, yes, but I also want to know why he can speak of his dead mother with such maturity when I can't stop conjuring the image of my dead sister. And I'm a selfish bitch for being jealous of his acceptance.

When I open my eyes again, he is looking at me with intent. His thumb moves to stroke my bottom lip and a tiny sigh escapes my throat. The table between us is quite narrow and there is so little distance keeping me from kissing him. It scares me. I feel like a bucket of ice water is being poured over my head and I snap back in my seat with such suddenness that I knock my bag over and the contents spill out on the floor under the table. Brady is still poised there with his hand extended, but the look on his face says he is disappointed. He recovers in record time and we both bend down to retrieve my things. I shove my clothing back in the bag and then I sit up too fast and smack the back of my head on the hard surface of the table. It stuns me and makes my vision swim for a minute, but I still see what is laying on the floor. The package I received earlier must not have been sealed properly because the contents have made their way onto the floor. The necklace my sister always wore, a platinum heart pendant with her Garnet birthstone in the center, is sticking out of the envelope. It is dirty; covered in a substance that I believe is dried blood, and a note is attached. The red lipstick from the mirror was used to spell out 'I will always find you'.

chapter eight

I hold an ice pack to the back of my head as I stare at Nicole's necklace. The one she was buried with. It is one of the only things I managed to hide from Brady as he pummeled me with question after question when we left the restaurant. I held my ground as firmly as I could and told him I need to go home and rest my head. I seriously doubt that he bought my explanation of an ex-boyfriend playing a sick joke. *I* don't even know what is going on.

I send off a quick text to Brady, letting him know I got home okay and that I will text him later. He insisted that he needed to spend the night at my place, on the couch of course, to make sure I didn't have a concussion. The only way I could get him to let me go home alone was to promise to text him every two hours. It is nice of him to be concerned, but I don't like the idea of having to check in with someone. That's part of the point of me coming here. I will just text him one more time before I go to sleep and then he's going to just have to deal. I didn't hit my head that hard and I think he knows that.

It has more to do with what he saw in that package and the fact that he knows I'm not telling the whole truth.

My sister was buried with this necklace. I keep saying it over and over in my mind like some kind of messed up mantra.

My sister was buried with this necklace.

My sister was buried with this necklace.

In the top drawer of my desk there is a false bottom. I feel around the edges until I snag the corner that only I know is there and I lift up. There is a knife with a mother of pearl handle, a Glock 29, and a small silver key. I take the key out, doing my best to avoid touching the gun, and I unlock the big drawer on the other side of the desk.

A photo album is the first thing I see and I pick it up. Nicole and I, much younger versions of ourselves, grace almost every page. I flip through to the last few years she was alive. In every photo after her fifteenth birthday, she is wearing this necklace. Our parents gave it to her that year and she loved it, refusing to take it off except for a few special occasions, like cleaning it or borrowing some of our mother's very expensive jewelry.

I put the album back and grab the thick file folder from the bottom. It's not in any particular order because I stole the file from my mother's home office and made copies before I took off. It takes a few minutes, but finally I close my fist around the paper I want triumphantly. This is the log of items that went into the casket with Nicole. I scan the list. Fourth form the top: platinum pendant with garnet inlay and platinum chain.

What kind of sick freak would dig up a dead girl and steal her necklace? Why send it to me? I don't have any answers, but I do feel a slow trickle of cold fear inch its way down my spine. I don't share my secrets with people. There isn't a soul in Miami that should know a thing about me or my sister. I know I haven't slipped up because up until a few days ago, I rarely spoke to anyone.

The number for the cemetery is listed here. They have to have surveillance cameras. I reach for my cell phone, but then I think better of it. If there was a disturbance, it would be a crime and would have to be reported. I'm better off looking that up instead because if I call there, I might look suspicious and phone calls can be traced. I can't let my parents find out where I am. They will think I'm losing my mind again and make me come home. That's not an option. I would rather die then go back to that hospital.

Two hours go by quickly, and I stop playing junior detective when the little alarm goes off on my phone to text Brady.

Still alive.

His response comes immediately. *Very funny. Two hours and text again. I'll be waiting.*

I wake up to pounding. My face is stuck to the papers on

the desk, and a tiny bit of saliva is crusted in the corner of my mouth. I wipe it off and grab my head. It throbs. I fell asleep in a very uncomfortable position and my neck aches as well. I just want the banging on my skull to go away.

Wait, that's not my head, it's the door. Someone is knocking on my apartment door? It's nearly impossible that anyone would have gotten in without calling up from security.

The spare bedroom that I use as my studying area is closer to the front door than my bedroom, so I answer the door without bothering to change from my pajamas. It's Brady. Of course it is. I should have known that he would do this if I didn't text him. I tend to underestimate how much people care about the well-being of others sometimes. Especially where I am concerned.

Brady moves around me and lets himself into my place before I have a chance to invite him in.

"Come right on in, then," I say, only slightly sarcastic, and gesture towards the couch dramatically.

He ignores me and puts one hand under my chin and tilts my face up so he can look at my eyes. "Your pupils aren't dilated, so that's good. You probably do not have a concussion."

I just stare at him. He drops his hands to his sides. "What? I majored in sports medicine before switching to Social Work."

"Why are you here, Brady? More importantly, how are

you here? I don't remember telling you where I lived, or telling security to let you upstairs."

He smirks. "I don't need security to call me in, I live here. Three floors down and on the other side of the hallway. I thought you knew that. We both arrived here at the same time after class on the first day. Jake, one of the front desk guys, is a good friend of mine. I told him about your head injury and he told me which unit you live in. Don't be mad."

I sigh. "I'm not mad. I just feel a little overwhelmed is all. I don't ever have people here, and certainly not at two in the morning."

Brady crosses his arms over his chest. I notice then that he's wearing sweatpants and a soft gray t-shirt that shows off just how powerful his body is. "If you had sent that text like you promised, I wouldn't have had to come and knock on your door in the middle of the night, would I?"

"I fell asleep. I was tired."

He stalks toward me as though I'm his prey. When he is inches away, he lowers his forehead to touch mine. "You hit your head hard on that table, Paige. I saw that you were dizzy. I don't know anything about what is going on with you and I know you're not going to tell me, but I'm not going to let you have no one to worry about you when you're hurt. I would like to know that you are okay. Okay?"

"Thank you, Brady. Really. I'm fine, though, so you can sleep knowing that I'll wake up in the morning."

He says nothing, just stares at me for another minute or two, and then moves to the couch and begins moving the throw pillows around.

"What are you doing?"

His reply is a bit muffled since he doesn't bother to turn around or look up. "I'm sleeping on the couch tonight. No arguing, it's happening. Would you mind grabbing me a blanket or something? Your apartment is an igloo."

An ironic smile touches my lips. "You wouldn't have said that a few hours ago. My air conditioning was busted. That's why I was out tonight. I didn't want to be here until it got taken care of."

He looks up, finally. "Really? How strange. They had the maintenance crew out here for that a week ago. Anything wrong should have been caught then."

I wave my hand in the air. "I abuse the hell out of the thermostat. I'm still not used to this heat and humidity so I run the thing constantly on full blast."

"It still shouldn't have had problems. This is a pretty new building. Too soon for things to start breaking down and needing repairs."

I look to the side and gesture with my arms as if presenting something. "Yeah, well, leave it to me to always get the shaft."

I have foot-in-mouth disease. I look at him and

immediately clasp my hand over my mouth, expecting the worst at any moment. Brady must have the worlds best poker face. His facial expression remains exactly as calm as it was before I started talking about shafts. I can't believe he isn't going to make fun of me at all.

And just when I think I'm getting away with that, he raises one eyebrow and says, "Yeah, well, I'm not going to touch that one."

chapter nine

We are at Turner's apartment for over an hour before I start to bug my sister about leaving for the dance. She clearly doesn't want to go, but I can tell she feels a bit guilty that I'm restless.

"Just a couple more minutes, Rebecca, I promise," she tells me and pats my leg as if to stay me.

"Maybe Turner could just come with us to the dance?" I ask.

Nicole shakes her head. "No, he went to school there a few years ago. The last thing I need is one of my teachers to recognize him and call Mama to tell her I'm with an older guy. Or any guy that isn't Justin."

Turner chimes in, and I dislike him even more. "What's wrong, Sweetie? I doubt you're dying to go to this school dance. You're determined to be a cock-block, aren't you? Keep reading that book and it will go by in no time."

I turn red and look back down at my phone, where I am using the electronic reader. Nicole gets up, abruptly, making both Turner and I jump. "Don't speak to her like that, Turner. Please apologize."

FROM YESTERDAY

Turner laughs. "What is the big deal? Are you kidding me right now? It was a joke."

I can tell when Nicole is becoming angry even if no one else can. There is a quiet fury in the way she holds herself; a rage that can erupt and yet be so elegant you never even realize she just took you down a few notches until much later. It is a gift. I can see this start to happen now. "Not a funny joke, Turner."

The way she sneers his name when she says it has so much disdain in it that I almost feel bad for him. The guy just went from being prime in her eyes, to the lowest form of scum on the bottom of her shoe and he knows it. He turns to look at me and I tremble. I have definitely ruined this guy's night. He puts a hand on Nicole's arm, still shooting dirty looks my way. "Sit down, Babe."

Nicole shrugs him off. "No. Apologize to Rebecca, and make it sound like you are very, very sorry. I don't let people speak to my sister that way."

"Okay, Nicole. You're right, I was out of line. Rebecca, I'm very sorry to have made you feel uncomfortable."

I don't say anything, I just nod my head to acknowledge the apology. I didn't want to come here and I don't want to be in the middle of an argument between them. Nicole picks her purse up off of the coffee table. Turner looks incredulous.

"What are you doing? I apologized."

Nicole smiles at him sweetly, grabs my hand, and walks us to the door. "I know. Good job with that. Now I'm going to take my little sister to the dance like I promised her and maybe, if you're lucky, I will call you tomorrow."

Tuner gets up and is on us instantly. He yanks Nicole's hand out of mine and pulls her to him. "Go back and sit down. I wasn't done talking to you yet." He faces me. "You can go watch TV in my bedroom."

I watch in stunned silence as Nicole tries to pull out of his grasp, but can't manage to extricate herself from the force of his hold. Turner throws the deadbolt on the front door and pulls her further into the living room. She struggles with him, but he still won't let her go. "Stop it, Turner, you're cutting off the circulation in my arm. Let go of me!"

"No, I don't think I'm going to do that. Get over here, Rebecca. I'm going to teach you bitches a lesson in how to respect a man and be a good guest."

I can't move. I don't know what is happening; I don't believe any of this is real. The only thing I can say with certainty right now is that my sister and I are in serious trouble.

"Paige."

"Mmmph."

"Paige, come on."

A tingling sensation creeps along my arm and I take my hand to slap whatever it is.

"Hey, that's not nice, Paige."

Suddenly, I'm aware that I'm not alone in my bedroom. I open my eyes and sit up so quickly that I'm dizzy from the effort.

"Brady? What are you doing in my bedroom?"

"We're not in your bedroom, Paige. As far as I know, this is your living room."

He's right. The heavy drapes are pulled over the windows so it is still dark in here, despite whatever time it is. My eyes are slowly adjusting to the darkness, but I can start to make out the furnishings in my living room. Why am I not in my bed? Wait, why am I in boy shorts and a tank top next to Brady on my couch? I pray that I don't have morning breath.

"I can see by the freaked out expression on your face that you don't remember falling asleep on the couch a few hours ago. Don't worry, you didn't snore, but you do have a tiny bit of a drooling issue."

Brady gestures to the corner of his mouth. My hand flies up to my own and I immediately try wiping non-existent saliva away. There's nothing there. The jerk starts laughing hysterically.

"Ha! I totally had you going. You should have seen your face. I really wish I'd taken a picture of that. Priceless."

"I'm kind of starting to hate you again, Brady. I really am."

He reaches over and pats me on the head like a little kid. "Come on, Paige, don't be sensitive. You look adorable in your little pink panties and top. Hot, actually. And remember that I'm here to make sure you don't slip into a coma from your little concussion earlier. I'm the good guy, right?"

His grin is irresistible, but I still feel like smacking him. "These are boy shorts, Brady, not panties. All women hate that word, by the way. And I do not have a concussion, for the last time. Nor am I sensitive."

I roll my eyes at him, but I can't resist flashing a small smile to show him I'm not angry. "What time is it?" I ask.

Brady looks at his phone. "Five thirty. Do you have classes today?"

"No. Do you?"

"I have Contemporary Lit at three this afternoon. I teach Spinning again at five. Interested?"

He looks hopeful and I do want to go. The question is, should I? Is this too much too soon? I have to limit how much of me he can see, and he already sees too much. He's very insightful, which will lead to him asking questions that I'd rather not answer.

"I'll try to make it, I just have some things I have to get done this afternoon."

Brady gets up and starts folding the blanket. "I'll give you some privacy, Paige. Thanks for indulging me and letting me know you were okay. Are you sure everything else is fine? Be honest."

He's terrible at folding a blanket so I take it from him and start refolding it into a rectangle, not whatever misshapen thing he was creating. "Yes, Brady, everything else is just fine."

At the door, he turns around before leaving and puts his hand on my arm, just under my shoulder. That familiar warmth starts to inch its way into my skin. "I know you're not telling me the truth about that envelope, Paige. I'm sure you are just trying to keep your business to yourself, and I respect that, but it's never a bad thing to ask for help. You can talk to me about anything, ok? I won't judge you, I promise."

I'm grateful that he doesn't wait for a response because I'm not sure I could speak without my emotion coming out in my voice right now. I close the door and lean against it. What have I gotten myself into?

Chapter Ten

I don't go to Brady's spinning class. I spend a good chunk of my morning staring at the necklace that was sent to me. I can't let go of the creepy feeling I get just from touching it. The packaging had my name and address on it, but no postage or return address. I suppose that makes sense since the guard did say it was sent by a private courier, and who would send such a sick thing to someone with no way to contact them? No one that I can think of. It's the kind of sick joke I'd almost expect Nicole to pull. That is, if my sister was still alive. She always did have a very twisted sense of humor.

Part of me feels like I should be scared to be in my apartment alone. First the lipstick; now this. They are not friendly gestures. The thing is, I'm not afraid. It's a particularly stupid way to feel when it's clear that someone wants me to be afraid. I should tell somebody, maybe take the evidence to the police.

Then I think, *evidence of what?* I washed the lipstick off of the mirror that very day and threw out that tube of it. The envelope from the necklace is tossed as well. Brady threw it out at the restaurant last night at my insistence. If I went to the cops, they would either laugh at me or start asking questions about who the necklace belonged to and that would lead back to my parents.

No.

Not an option.

I'm a big girl, and I can take care of myself.

Finally, around two o' clock, I make myself get up and I go to campus to get some studying done. I stop in the food court area and grab a coffee and a veggie wrap, stuff it into my bag so I can get into the library, and go find a nice secluded spot on the third floor. For some reason, no one ever comes up here, it's as quiet as can be. The hours fly by as I study for a Calculus exam that is being so thoughtfully administered on the first day of the second week of school. Calculus is just so much fun and so very easy. Or not, but it does manage to distract me for a while until I look at my watch and notice it is 5:15 and I am missing the cycling workout. I feel a tiny twinge of regret; I do enjoy seeing Brady in workout gear with sweat gleaming all over that body, but it's probably for the best. I don't need him thinking I'm so obsessed with him that I'll show up everywhere he is at anytime. Absence makes the heart grow fonder and all of that.

I really have to stop thinking about Brady in any kind of capacity that could include something other than casual friendship.

It is still light outside by the time I walk back from the library. I try not to walk alone at night, because it is a long stretch of dark road that could prevent a driver from seeing me or conceal an axe murderer in all the shrubbery and trees. Also, I'm not that stupid. When the time changes, though, I'll ahve to come back earlier because it will be dark by 6, which is the time now.

"Good evening," I call out to the front desk guard as I walk through the lobby.

"Evening, Miss Kerimov."

He nods and smiles at me and I give a small smile in return before stepping on to the elevator.

My phone goes off, signaling that I have a new text message as I'm riding up to my floor, but I ignore it for the moment. I kind of feel like ordering Thai takeout, despite the fact that I ate it last night and that particular meal didn't have such great memories for me. Or, it kind of did, but it didn't end quite as well as it began.

When I step off of the elevator, I see Elyse's red mane disappearing into her apartment. I wait a minute before getting completely out of the car; the doors try to close twice, and then I breathe a sigh of relief that I missed her. I am going to dinner at her place next week, but that doesn't mean I have to chat with her all the time. It would be too much.

I turn the key in the lock and that feeling of unease starts to prick it's way back into my skin. First my arms develop gooseflesh, and then the chill starts to caress the back of my neck. There is something not right here. A sane person would not go inside, I think, but this is just me being ridiculous. No one has a key to my place other than the landlord, who spends the entire summer in Italy, so he's not even in the country right now. Nor has he ever violated my privacy by dropping in unannounced. There's no one here.

Just to double check, I go through the apartment to each room and glance in to make sure.

Not a soul.

I walk my paranoid ass into my office and start looking for the takeout menu to the Thai place. I've almost located it when I hear a creaking noise, and then the distinct sound of a door handle being turned. The only place in this condo that makes a sound like that is the guest bathroom right across from this spare room. Chills breaking out across my body again, I very quietly walk to the door of this room, grabbing the three foot tall pillar candle off of it's base as I go. I think better of it and take the base instead; it is much heavier.

Then the front door closes and I know for sure that is the sound I heard because that door is very heavy and it slams if you let go of it, but if you don't it has a loud clicking noise as it sets in place. I hear the click. I rush out of the spare bedroom and no longer terrified, I run to the entrance and out into the hall.

There is no one there.

Impossible, I know I heard someone. Both elevators are resting on the first floor and there is no way they had time to get that far, nor could they have reached the stairwell without me seeing them first.

No. No. No.

I won't start questioning my sanity, not this time. I'm sure my ears didn't deceive me. I am not crazy.

I am not crazy.

I run back to my apartment and slam the door shut behind me. I feel frantic; sweat pours down over my forehead and into my eyes making them sting. A feeling of complete helplessness shudders through me and I cave; giving in to the doubt and shame of the people who were supposed to love me. The things they said I did, the things they told me I made up; I let myself believe it. It crushes me with the memory of a locked door and a room with white walls and no windows.

A knock on the door brings me back to myself and as quickly as I lost control, I regain it. A look through the peep hole and I breathe a sigh of releif so big the air could last me for an entire month. I open the door and fling myself into the arms of a very surprised Brady.

"Paige, what's going on? Are you okay?"

Not trusting my voice, I simply nod against his chest and I practically wilt like a tattered doll as he hugs me a little tighter and walks us both into the foyer.

I breathe in his scent once more before I pull away and step back.

"Not that I mind, Paige, but what just happened? And don't say nothing because you are the most resistant of any girl I have ever met and you're flushed and sweaty. You look like you saw a ghost."

I shake my head. "Can we please just not talk about it? I just, I'm having a bad day is all."

I turn and head to the living room without waiting for a reply, knowing he will just follow me without an invitation inside.

And I am right, because he's practically at my heels. "No way, Paige. You have to tell me something. I promise I will not judge you. If you need help, you can ask me. You know that right?"

I whirl around to face him and angrily hold my right hand up in the air. "I don't need any help, Brady. I just need you to be my friend and not ask so many questions, okay? Can you please just--"

I don't finish my sentence when I see what's been left for me in front of the couch. I missed it before because you have to walk around the couch from the hall to sit down.

There is a doll with features eerily similar to my own laying there, and a gun is positioned in her hand with what looks like blood extending out from the gun and covering a large area of the rug. Like the pool of blood you might find next to the body of someone who had been shot in the head.

    The gun is mine.

FROM YESTERDAY

chapter eleven

Between dodging Elyse and trying to dissuade Brady from asking more questions about the terrifying little doll and the gun in my apartment, Saturday feels like the best thing that ever happened to me. I sleep until ten thirty. When I am finally awake, I remain in bed and enjoy the quiet calm of my bedroom. When I go to sleep on Friday or Saturday night, I leave my phone in another room so that calls, texts, or anything else that may make my phone go off can't bother me. I don't think it's good to be available every moment of your life.

Finally, around noon, I shower and get myself dressed. I've got plenty of studying to do today and I'd like to get it done in time to watch the Ohio State game at 7. One of the few good memories I have from back home is watching college football with my father and Nicole when we were little. My parents met at Ohio State, and although American football isn't big in Ukraine, my father loves it. I think he tried very hard to make himself fit in to American culture as much as possible, given that the conditions he grew up in were less than desirable. If it had not been for my grandmother meeting an American business man by chance about two years after she was widowed, my father would have stayed there and lived a very different life. And, while not really in the same league, I can understand how difficult it is to move to a completely new place at the age of eighteen, where you don't know anyone. At least I know the language. He did not.

Before heading to the library, I make a phone call that I desperately need to make.

"This is Kelly Sullivan."

I take a deep breath. "Dr. Sullivan, it's me."

I hear some shuffling noises, and a muttered curse. "Hold on. Do not hang up. I just need to go somewhere a bit more private, okay?"

"I'm not hanging up," I say.

A few minutes of muffled noises and she returns. "I've been worried about you, Kid. I didn't expect you to just run off like that and not tell anyone where you went. Is everything okay?"

"Honestly, I don't know. Some strange things have been happening lately."

There is a pause, and I can practically hear her thinking. "Remember what I told you? You have to remove yourself from the situation before you get overwhelmed by the memory of someone that is no longer here. Your perception of Nicole is still skewed, Kid. I told you from the get go, you can't idealize people, no matter how much you love them. When you think of your sister, picture her as person with real flaws, just like everyone else. You still get too caught up in the way she was as a sister, and who she was to everyone else."

I sigh. "I try. I really do. It's just that sometimes, I miss her so much that I want to pretend she's still here so it won't hurt so much."

"I know it's hard, but you have to concentrate on your own well-being now. You have to have a life, and she can't be such a big part of it or you'll never really move on. And you haven't yet, have you?"

"No, Dr. Sullivan. Sometimes I think I have, and I'll go days feeling normal, but then someone or something reminds me of her and it hurts all over again."

"Can you tell me where you are, Kid? Do you need me to come to you?"

Oh, god. A pain in my chest, an ache so deep that I didn't realize it was possible, begins to squeeze and throb. I want to see someone familiar, someone that cared about me back home, I want it badly, but I can't risk it.

"No," I tell her. "Thank you, but I think it's best if I just try to take your advice and keep the past in the past."

"Okay, Kid. I'm glad you called. Don't worry about a thing, it's still doctor-patient privilege regardless of the fact that you are no longer in this place. I can't say a word to your parents, but please, I want you to call me at any time if you need anything at all. I will always be available to you, you got that? That's why I gave you my personal cell phone number."

"You don't know how much that means to me, Dr. Sullivan."

Before I change my mind and take her up on her offer, I hang up.

The phone call to Dr. Sullivan took a lot longer than I expected and now I have to hurry up if I want to make the one o' clock cycling class before the library. I called the gym to make sure the scheduled instructor was going to be there and there wasn't going to be a surprise substitute in the form of Brady. I just need to make it through the day in solitude. It will help get me back on track. '

I throw a change of clothes into by gym bag, check to make sure my shower stuff is in there, pull my hair up into a bun and I'm out the door. Elyse is in the hall with a man that I presume to be the fiance.

"Paige! Oh, great. You can finally meet Garrett."

Damn. I thought this guy was out of town until Monday. So much for my quick escape. Garrett smiles and puts his hand out for me to shake.

"Nice to meet you, Paige. Elyse hasn't stopped talking about you since I got back."

FROM YESTERDAY

Garrett is very tall, probably 6' 5" or so. It's a good thing Elyse is quite tall herself. They look good together. Elyse even looks happier than the few times I've seen her before. Probably because she's not alone in a strange city anymore.

"Nice meeting you as well. I hate to run off so quickly, but I have a test coming up and hours of studying."

Elyse smiles. "Of course, Paige. We'll see you Tuesday. Oh, and bring that completely hot guy I saw over here the other night."

She winks at me and Garrett doesn't bat an eyelash when she mentions another man. That's always a good sign in a partner. I think.

"I'm not sure he can make it, but I'll ask him," I lie.

There is no way I'm asking Brady to come for dinner, I think to myself as I ride the elevator downstairs. It would seem too much like a double date. Yet, the idea of having someone else there so that I'm not on my own with two people that I don't really know, well, it is appealing. Not that I know Brady so much better; I met him a few days ago. Oddly, it feels like I do, though. He's become the only source of familiarity to me and I like it.

I took too long getting my act together so I have to take my car instead of walking to the campus. Now that I've seen it, I notice the motorcycle Brady took me on only two rows and one stall away from my car. One of those stupid smiles is on my face before I even realize it. All from looking at a bike.

I'm a smitten idiot.

Nicole would be so proud.

I pull in to the first spot I see near the student center and jog over to the gym. I manage to throw my stuff inside a locker and get to the cycling class just in time. It's a good class, but the instructor doesn't quite inspire me the way Brady did, which is no surprise since I don't have a crush on this girl.

After a quick shower, I throw on some yoga pants and a t-shirt with Hello Kitty on the front. Childish, maybe, but I just don't think you are ever too old for Hello Kitty. Nicole used to love teasing me about my thing for Hello Kitty, even when I was young enough for it to be acceptable. She never did enjoy playing with dolls; perhaps my sister was far too grown up for her own good.

The library is surprisingly quiet for a Saturday afternoon and I have no trouble finding my quiet little corner on the third floor. I spread my books out on the table, open my laptop, and get my headphones out of my bag. Portishead pours out of the tiny speakers; Beth Gibbons' voice like liquid silk. I find my rhythm and lose myself to the intimidating equations from my trig class. An hour or more goes by without me noticing a single person come up here. I love the third floor.

Another half hour passes when I feel the effect of the two water bottles I drank at the gym. I grab my purse, but leave my laptop and my books on the table. No one will take anything, not that anyone is here, and I will be gone for two minutes. The desk I'm sitting at is all the way in the back where there are no windows, so I'm a bit surprised to see that it is dark outside when I get to the restroom. I'm glad I took my car. I use the bathroom quickly and step back into the main room. Is it my imagination, or is something different? It just feels a bit off. It's like that feeling you get when a light goes out in a room with many bulbs, so it's not immediately obvious what changed, but you just know there is a difference.

Cautiously, I approach the table that holds my belongings. Everything looks to be in its place as I left it, but I can't shake the eerie vibe I felt a moment ago. The quiet of the third floor is starting to lose its appeal. If things hadn't been so weird for me the past few days, I would tell myself to stop being such a baby and get back to work. The thing is, *something* has been going on. I can't pretend like it hasn't. Either way, I have to study for this test.

Once my headphones are back in place, I calm down and forget all about the uneasiness I am experiencing. Something in my peripheral vision moves and it startles me. I look up, but I don't see anything or anyone.

Now you're just making this stuff up, I tell myself.

Then, just a moment later, I see something move again from the corner of my eye. Glancing slowly to my left, I see a pile of old reference books on the floor where I know they weren't there when I came in. The books are in a pile in front of the staircase; I would have had to have stepped over them when I arrived. I turn my music off. It must have been too loud, damn those noise-canceling ear buds, for me to hear the books fall.

Those books didn't fall, though. Right there out in the open, there was no bookshelf for them to fall off of. I'm done here. I start shoving my stuff into my bag as quickly as I can manage. I run towards the stairs, but the second I reach the tile, my feet go out from under me. I go down hard, catching my arm on something sharp on the way. I feel the skin rip and pain, so swift and intense, overloads my senses and, mercifully, I lose consciousness.

FROM YESTERDAY

Chapter Twelve

Turner moves with lightening-quick speed. Neither Nicole nor I see the blow coming, just a blur of movement and a cracking sound before Nicole is down. She becomes an unconscious mass of limp arms and legs with a purplish knot forming on the right side of her forehead. My brain stops firing synapses and my body glues itself to the floor as if welcoming Turner to make his next move. He turns his head away from my sister and his gaze falls on me. Where is my fight or flight instinct? Flight would be good right now. Run. Run to a neighbor and get help for Nicole, *I tell myself.*

An unsettling snarl mars Turner's handsome face. "You wouldn't get far, Princess. Trust me."

Truth, unlike any I have heard in the past, is what my ears pick up from his words. I can reason that my diminutive stature would give me an advantage speed wise, but that deadbolt is at least half a foot higher than I am and Turner's body is hard edges and solid muscle.

Like a panther stalking his prey, Turner advances until the air I breathe is nothing but mouthwash and cologne. The coat closet door opens and I am urged forward into the dark, empty little cell by a hand to the back of my neck.

"Sit," he commands.

Inch by inch, my legs lower me down as I look upward and beg for leniency with the silent pleading of eye-contact. Above me, Turner reaches for an item on the top shelf and when I see his hand come back with several plastic zip ties, my blood becomes the temperature of Lake Michigan in a snow storm.

"Hands behind your back, Princess. Now."

Why? Why am I complying? Am I really this weak? Can't I at least try and put up a fight? I have watched my big sister stand up for herself for years. I could follow her example.

Instead I clasp my hands behind my back and allow myself to be tied up by bits of plastic that dig into my wrists.

"Now, be a very quiet little girl and I won't have to knock you out like I did Nicole. Make a sound, Princess, and I promise it will be your last."

He steps back and closes the door.

No.

There isn't a sliver of light, not even from under the door. The closet, already tiny, gets increasingly smaller as my breathing starts to pick up speed until I am gasping for air. My chest gets tight and it feels like my heart is going to explode. I open my mouth to scream, but before I can get the sound out of my throat and seal my fate, logic comes back to me. I can't make noise; I don't know Turner well enough to know if he will follow through on his threat, but I'm not *stupid enough to test him. Clearly, he isn't a very stable person. And if I die now, what will happen to my sister? Surely, if Turner were to kill me, he would not leave a witness around to nail him.*

I watch every version of Law and Order and this is the best I can come up with? I need to figure out how to get us out of here.

By the sounds coming from outside the closet door, I better figure it out fast.

The pain in my arm jolts me awake. The first thing I see is the blond guy from the circulation desk standing over me and holding up two fingers in front of my face.

"Can you see this? How many fingers am I holding up?"

Gingerly, I try to raise myself to a sitting position, but can't. I settle for smacking the guy's hand out of my face. "I can see just fine."

Blond Guy places his hand on my shoulder with the good arm and gently applies pressure. "I don't think you should try to get up yet. You fell really hard; I heard the thud all the way downstairs. Why don't you lie there for a moment while I get something soft for your head? I'll call an ambulance, too."

I sit up so fast my head spins and I reach out to grab him. "No! No ambulance! Please?"

He holds his hands up in mock surrender. "Whoa, Spaz, calm down. Okay, no ambulance. Let me see your arm."

I twist to the side and lean back against the foot of the

staircase. Blond guy gingerly lifts my arm and we both glance at it. You know how you don't feel the full extent of your injuries until you look directly at them? It is all I can do to keep from passing out again. Even this guy starts looking a little pale when he sees the torn flesh that runs almost the entire length of my forearm; jagged, angry, inflamed. It definitely needs stitches.

"That's gross. You need to have that looked at, Paige. And not just by a lowly pre-med student like me. A real doctor who can clean that out and stitch it up."

A warning bulb lights up in my head. "How did you know my name was Paige?"

He gives me a disgusted look. "Uh, I don't know. Maybe because we had three classes together Freshman year? We sat next to each other in Bio 2, second semester, remember?"

My arm hurts so badly I can't even pretend to know what his name is. I can sort of recall seeing him in a class or two, but I never really look people in the eye. I just look at him now, and give him a half grimace.

Sympathy washes away the hurt look he had a moment ago. "It's okay. My name is Alex. I shouldn't have expected you to know that. It's not like we ever introduced ourselves. I just paid more attention to you because you're so quiet. I don't think I heard you speak once, actually. Also, you're pretty."

Alex blushes and looks away. I am in too much pain to process this right now. "I, uh, I really need a towel or something."

He jumps up. "Oh! Sorry. The first aid kit. I'll be back in a second. Don't go anywhere."

I give him a pointed look and he goes down the stairs.

I close my eyes and count to one hundred before Alex gets back. When he does return, he is running up the stairs so quickly that he nearly slips and ends up with the same fate as me, but he rights himself at the last second. Good, because two down and no one to go equals not so great odds for us both. I'm sitting here seriously contemplating the ambulance now that I realize I can barely move, let alone stand and walk to the car *and* drive home.

"Did you slide through this oil, too? Is that how you fell, or was it from carrying those heavy books?"

Alex sets the first aid kit down next to me as he finishes asking inane questions.

"Oil? What? I wasn't carrying those books. They fell just before I left. That's *why* I was leaving."

"No, look, Paige. Your shoes."

I glance in the direction of my feet without moving too much. He's right. There are what look like oil stains on the side of my right sneaker and traveling up a bit on to the gray sweatpants. Now I notice the puddle that sits less than two feet away from me; part of it has been tracked through by both me and Alex.

"That's odd."

Alex gives me an incredulous look. "Odd? That's all you have to say about it? And the books, Paige? How did you expect to manage all of that, plus your school bag? Reference books can't be checked out, you know?"

"Uh, thanks. I'm aware of that. I just told you the books are what freaked me out. I didn't drop them. Whomever else was up here must have."

Alex begins to gently wrap some gauze around my arm. It stings, but I try not to complain.

"There was no one up here besides you, Paige. I've been at the circulation desk since before you got here. I came up here once to get a Physiology textbook, and you were still the only person here. I haven't left the desk since then."

I'm starting to feel annoyed. "Well, Alex, maybe it was a ghost."

I say it ironically, but the truth is that I'm not so certain that I'm wrong, which is ridiculous.

Alex gently secures the bandage with a small piece of medical tape and stands back up. "All kidding aside, Paige, there was no oil on the floor earlier and those big ass books didn't get up and drop themselves on the floor. Plus, that arm. It has to get looked at right now. I can't try to clean it properly without a local anasthetic. The pain would be off the charts. I'm not allowed to leave, so you'll either go to the hospital in an ambulance or you can call someone to take you. Your choice."

He folds his arms over his chest and I know he's not going to budge.

Too weak to argue, I acquiesce. "Fine. Can you get my cell out of the side pocket in my bag, please? I'll call someone."

There is only one person for me to call.

Chapter Thirteen

"Fuck, Paige! What the hell happened?"

Brady must have been on campus, nearby, because less than five minutes later he is assessing the situation with Alex.

"It's not as bad as it looks," I lie to him.

He shakes his head while Alex feels the need to chime in. "Yes, it is. Brady, right? She needs to go to an ER or urgent care immediately. That's a very nasty, very deep cut that needs antibiotics and stitches. And she will also need a tetanus shot if she isn't up to date."

Brady and Alex have a two minute whispered conversation while I lay there and imagine what kinds of conspiracy theories Alex is telling him. I wish they would stop, I don't need more people thinking that I'm crazy.

Brady shakes Alex's hand. "Thanks for helping, man. I've got it from here."

"No problem. You take care of yourself, Paige."

FROM YESTERDAY

Alex watches as Brady bends down and uses brute strength to scoop me up from the floor and into his arms like a new bride on her honeymoon. Lovely as his arms might be, there is no chance in hell I'm going anywhere like this. Plus, I didn't like the little exchange that just happened between the two boys. I feel like a piece of property now.

I smack Brady's arm with my good one. "No way, Tarzan. I'll walk."

He lets me down, but won't let go of my uninjured arm as we make our way down the steps. My bag sways on his shoulder and one of the straps comes around to tap me right over the area that hurts. I yelp.

"Damn, I'm sorry."

He shifts the bag to this other side and we make it to my car with relative ease.

"I'll drive your car, Paige. I came here on the bike and you're not going to the ER on that."

For once, we are in complete agreement. "The keys are in that side compartment, next to my phone."

He digs around for a second until he pulls them out and unlocks the passenger door for me. Once he has me settled in with my seatbelt in place, he makes his way around to the driver's side. I have to be a little bit impressed when Brady is able to adjust the seat without fumbling around for the controls like most people. My car has buttons in very illogical places and it can take some getting used to. I can tell he's a bit shocked that my car does not have an automatic transmission; I've found that most Americans, both genders, don't know how to drive stick these days. It's weird to me, but I guess that's because my parents were not raised here. I'm used to the fact that there are many countries in which stick shift is the norm and automatic is a very rare luxury.

The ride to the hospital is relatively quick; it is literally five minutes down from campus on Biscayne Boulevard, but traffic makes it take closer to ten. We don't speak during this time. I am not exactly in the position to be having a meaningful conversation right now, and to my relief it seems as though Brady is as perceptive as he is pushy. The silence is a companionable one; we are both content to simply be in one another's presence. It's nice.

Aventura Hospital is over ten stories high and all chrome and glass, having been updated just a few years ago. This is one of the nicer areas in South Florida. The city is small, but packed with high rises and expensive cars. The traffic backs all the way up to the area I live in, which is only one city away, really. Brady parks my car in the garage, which looks fairly empty. I hope this translates to not having to wait nine hours in the ER since I'm not an urgent case.

We walk inside and the triage nurse assesses me quickly. We are told to have a seat, but that it shouldn't be long before I am called in. There are the usual uncomfortable plastic chairs for us to sit in.

" You know, you don't have to wait," I tell Brady. "You're

welcome to take my car home and I can just take a cab home when I'm done."

Brady rolls his eyes at me. "Yeah, sure, Paige. I'll just leave you here. In the emergency room. By yourself."

"It's not a big deal, Brady. I'm perfectly fine. This could take hours and I'd hate for you to give up your Saturday night to hang out with me in the hospital."

He puts his hand on my knee. "Paige, I'm not giving anything up. I was even going to see what your plans were for the evening. So, whether we are here the rest of the night, or somewhere else, I'll be just fine. Now, tell me about what happened in the library."

Before I can figure out a way not to tell him very much, my name is called by the nurse. "I guess I'll have to tell you when I come back out."

Brady stands up. "Oh, I'm coming in with you. We can talk about it later if you want, but we will talk about it."

"Later sounds good."

chapter fourteen

Three hours, two doctors, some shots, and fourteen stitches later and I am finally home. Brady is hovering over me as I chill out on the couch. I like it.

"Okay, so The Hunger Games or Bridesmaids?"

I laugh. "Do you really want to watch a chick flick? You don't seem like the type. The Hunger Games is good."

Brady frowns at me. "I'll have you know that I have watched plenty of chick flicks. Especially if I was trying to get laid."

I toss a throw pillow at him. "Nice. Well, just so *you* know, that is not happening. So don't get your hopes up."

"Relax, Paige. I was teasing. Mostly. Why don't we just watch both? It's only 9 o' clock. The sushi won't be here for at least a half hour so we can start a movie, or you can tell me how you really hurt yourself today."

I hold out my hand and wait for Brady to grab it. When he does, I squeeze his hand and look at him. "Brady, I'm still not feeling great and I'd be lying if I said that I'm not still a little freaked out over the whole thing. All I really want to do is spend a few hours with my friend, watching movies and forgetting about today. I promise I will tell you, I just want to try and salvage what is left of this evening, okay?"

He nods and continues to hold my gaze. "Just as long as I'm this friend you are talking about."

He winks.

I drop his hand. "Take a look around, Brady. Do you see anyone else here? Let's watch The Hunger Games first. I have a girl crush on Jennifer Lawrence, just like half of the rest of the female population."

You can almost see the cartoon light bulb flash above his head. He raises one eyebrow, a trick that is not easy. "Oh, really? That has numerous possibilities, Paige. I like it"

"Sure you do, perv. What possibilities would those be, exactly? I'm never going to meet her and even if I did, we are both straight. And who's to say I'm *her* type?"

He seems undeterred. "Still, it's hot to imagine..."

I don't let him finish his thought because I beam him with another throw pillow. I'm going to run out of pillows soon. I suppose we could make popcorn. Plenty of that to throw.

Brady puts the movie in the blu-ray player and then settles on the couch next to me. He hits play on the remote, and then moves himself closer and examines my arm. He turns it to the side to get a better look.

"The bandage needs to be changed soon, Paige. There's still some bleeding. Do you want to take some of the meds they gave you?"

"No, not really. It's just naproxen 500 so it won't help that much. I'd rather tough it out. I can change the bandage later."

Brady takes hold of my wrist. "Let me change the bandage now so that you don't worry about staining your couch. I promise to be gentle. And I really think you should take one of the pills, they will help with the inflammation."

I shrug. "Fine, but pause the movie first, please? I don't want to miss the scene when Katniss volunteers for her sister."

Brady grins. He pauses the disc, even though we are still on previews, and goes to get the bag of bandages they gave me at the hospital. It is going to be really interesting trying to shower later. I hurt my right arm and I am right handed. The doctor told me not to get it wet for a few days which means a plastic covering and awkward movements while trying to wash my hair.

Brady comes back with supplies; there is gauze, antiseptic, and medical tape in the cellophane bag with care instructions on the side. He reads that for a minute, then sets everything down on the coffee table and sits back down next to me.

"Okay, give me your arm."

I lift it, realizing that the anesthetic is starting to wear off. Maybe the naproxen is a good idea after all. "I changed my mind. I do want to take one pill."

He looks pleased. "Good. I'll do this quickly and then grab some water for you."

I grab the bottle of pills and toss one into my mouth. I dry swallow a pill the size of a horse tranquilizer in no time. "No need."

Brady's eyes are the size of saucers. "That was disturbing. And, uh, kind of hot all at the same time. Anyway, I'm just going to slowly pull this bandage off, clean the wound very gently, and re-bandage it, okay?"

I hold my arm out. "Sure."

With extreme care and gentleness, Brady pulls the bandage off of my arm bit by bit. The skin underneath is rust-colored from the iodine and it looks grotesque where the stitches have pulled the skin together like ruched fabric. Bits of dried blood have flaked off and they fall on to the towel that Brady thoughtfully placed on the couch before starting. He throws the ruined bandage into a plastic bag and picks up the antiseptic. "This is probably going to sting."

I nod. "I'm sure."

It takes less than thirty seconds for Brady to uncap the solution, spread it on some gauze, and press down gingerly on my arm. The pain is quick, like a short, intense burst of sensations that dissipate soon after. Reminds me of the first time I got my bikini line waxed. Before I know it, he has replaced the old bandage with a new one and it's over.

"There. All set. How bad was it?"

I hold his hand for the second time today. "Thank you. For everything."

He doesn't need clarification. Brady knows there is much more meaning in my words than simply thanking him for changing the dressing on my arm. I feel very lucky to have found a friend like him, regardless of whether or not I wanted one.

"You may be thanking me now, but it'll be me who is giving thanks later."

I watch the evil grin form on his face. "Oh? Why is that?"

He winks. "Because you've injured your right arm and you are right-handed. So, I'll have to change that dressing for you for the next few days because it has to stay clean. And if you think you'll be able to shower without my help, you are so very wrong."

An once again, I am rendered speechless. There is simply no good comeback for that. He is right.

I grab the remote from the table and press play. Brady laughs quietly to himself. We watch until just after my favorite scene when the phone rings. It is the front desk, calling to have me authorize the delivery man inside the building. I tell him yes, and then I go to find my purse to get cash ready.

"Don't worry about it, Paige. I've got it."

"Like hell. You paid for dinner the other night, and you dragged my injured butt to the emergency room today. The least I can do is buy dinner."

I locate my wallet and give a triumphant yell as I pull it from my bag just as the delivery man knocks on the door. Brady comes over to me, takes my wallet, and shoves it into his back pocket. "You're never going to pay when I'm around. Ever. Better start getting used to it now."

I watch, open-mouthed, as he goes to the door, opens it, and pays the man. When he finishes, he takes the huge box of take-out into the living room and sets it down on the coffee table. We both work quietly, setting up a little picnic of sorts, while I ponder why I'm slightly turned on by having Brady order me around.

"I am perfectly capable of paying for stuff, Brady."

He gestures with his hands around the room. I take a minute to follow where his fingers go as he points to my rather expensive furnishings and the detail that went into the finishes in the condo. All modern furniture, mostly dark wood with clean lines. I have very few decorations, not being one for clutter, but the items I do have were not cheap. And sitting on the end table is a genuine Swarovski crystal vase.

"Take a look around you, Paige. I know you can afford it, as could anyone that lives in this building. Which, if you recall, includes me. So just deal with it."

I glare at him, determined not to let him think I'm okay with his macho attitude, but the truth is I am very attracted to this side of him. There is definitely something wrong with me.

We return to the movie and dig into our dinner. The next hour or so is spent with us watching and stuffing our mouths. At one point, Brady opens a box with dynamite rolls and after taking a bite of one, he reaches towards my mouth with his chopsticks. "Here," he says. "You have to try this."

I don't blink an eye at the fact that a guy who is not my boyfriend is feeding me a piece of half-eaten sushi. I just take the piece from his chopsticks with my mouth, keeping eye contact between us. It is good. I even make a very audible, involuntary groan as we continue to stare at one another. Before I even have a chance to be embarrassed by it, I see Brady close his eyes for a moment, as if he's pained by something. When he brings one finger to my mouth and runs it over the corner of my lips, I shiver.

The nights I've spent between the day we met and now tossing and turning in my sleep. The extra steps I am taking these days which put me directly in his path, knowing or unknowingly, just to see him for a moment. The lies I let fall off my lips when I deny the most basic human desire there is.

I could say something right now. My voice could break the barrier that is more than just sound between our bodies.

His fingers on my face, his elbow resting gently near my

breastbone, our knees gently intertwined. My hands, limp at my sides, ache to reach for him and slide down each one of his arms. A few inches to my right and I could taste him; even a chaste, close-mouthed kiss would wake me up. I don't notice that Brady has been closing the gap between us, ever so slowly, until a fraction of an inch is all that is left to cross.

"Don't."

A stranger's voice escapes from the very treacherous vocal cords I call my own. Eons stretch between the time I was last comfortable in my skin, before I folded everything that made me a person into a neat little box and taped it shut, to this new person that lets her guard down once in a while. That one word should have stayed stuffed down deep; instead the languidness of the moment shifts into a rigid resignation.

Brady barely moves, yet his body is all of sudden much farther away than it was a moment ago. He does his best to keep an even expression on his face, but his eyes have a hint of disappointment in them that may or may not be transference from my own.

"I'm sorry."

The apology pours out of me, but the set of his jaw doesn't soften and the hurt thickens his voice. "Don't be. I should probably go. You need to rest."

My stomach churns with regret as he talks about leaving. "We didn't talk about what happened in the library."

Oh, good job, Paige. Way to bring that up now so that you

can't keep avoiding it, I think.

Brady shakes his head. "You don't want to talk about that. You aren't big on sharing much of yourself, Paige. I wish you would tell me what's going, I really do, but I'm not going to push you anymore. It isn't fair to either one of us."

I look at him, unable to use my words. This is the same person that pushed his way into my life with brute force? The ache that began to form in my chest a moment ago deepens.

He stands up and tips my chin up towards him with his right hand. "Don't look at me like that, Paige. I'm not giving up on you. It's just going to have to be you who makes an effort, okay? You know where I am."

He reaches the front door of my apartment before I have time to process all the emotions swirling around in my head.

"Don't forget to keep that bandage clean and dry. Call me if you need anything, Paige."

The door shuts behind him and I feel more alone than I have in years.

chapter fifteen

Sunday morning is as bleak as I feel, with a gray sky and rain so heavy that visibility is only a few feet in front of you. I love staying inside on days like this. Watching a good thunderstorm has always been a favorite thing of mine. When Nicole was alive, we would pop popcorn and sit outside under the covered deck in our backyard to watch the storms. My parents would shake their heads, but they left us alone as long as there wasn't a lightening storm. It was usually Malvina that finally ushered us inside, telling us that her heart couldn't handle it anymore.

Nicole would have loved Florida. Ohio saw its fair share of summer storms, but Florida is a mecca for unpredictable weather. Someone told me once that if you don't like the weather in Miami, just go down the street. And it is so very true because I was out jogging once and I could actually see it raining a few blocks from where I was, but it remained dry as could be where I was.

I make some coffee and draw the blinds open in the living

room. I'm tempted to just go out onto the balcony, but the throbbing in my arm reminds me that I'm not allowed to get the wound wet.

Fantastic, I think. *How am I going to shower without help?*

Maybe I should have just let Brady kiss me. Then he'd still be here to take care of me. He has proven to be really good at that so far. The thing is, I shouldn't need or want anyone to do that for me. Why did I pull away, though, when it was so obvious that I was as into it as he was? I'm not frigid; I have been intimate with other men in the past.

There is a knock at the door and my stomach leaps. Brady! I set my coffee cup down on the breakfast bar and rush to the door. I'm glad I slept in form-fitting black leggings and tank top last night because I actually feel kind of sexy in this. Despite the messy hair I must be sporting.

When I open the door, I try to hide my disappointment when I see that it is Elyse, not Brady, who has come by this morning.

"Hey, Paige. I hope I'm not interrupting you."

I give her a half smile. "No, you're not. How are you?"

I stop myself just short of asking her what she's doing here. I'm working on not being rude.

Elyse's face falls just slightly before she catches herself and puts her usual smile back in place. "Garrett was called away for work really early this morning. I was making him a really great brunch, but now it's going to waste so I thought maybe you would want to eat it with me?"

She holds up a plastic container and I instantly smell baked goods. I'd be a fool to turn that down, so I step back and give Elyse room to come inside.

"Thank you. Come in."

She walks into the kitchen and sets the food on the counter. "Where do you keep your plates?"

I grab two plates from the cabinet over the dishwasher machine. The drawer with utensils is on the other side of the breakfast nook. I grab some forks and a serving spoon and then head over to the stool next to Elyse.

"That's a huge gauze pad, Paige. And you've bled right through it. What happened?"

Great. I forgot all about yesterday and didn't even think to throw a sweatshirt on. "It's no big deal. The floor in the library had some slippery stuff on it and I'm clumsy. I fell and hit the corner of something on the way down. Just a few stitches, nothing serious."

The look on Elyse's face said she thought it was a bigger deal than I was making it into. Which was exactly what I would like to avoid. Of course, I have a great way to distract her.

"Actually, Elyse, I know we just met and all, but how would you feel about seeing me naked?"

I wish I could take a picture of her expression when I ask this. It is priceless.

"I, uh, what?"

I giggle. "I'm not supposed to get the wrapping wet and I really want to shower. I just need some help making sure I keep my arm dry while I'm in there. Oh, wow. You made all of this? It looks like it came straight out of a magazine."

Out of the box, Elyse has produced cheese croissants, scrambled eggs, and some kind of pastry with what looks like raspberry filling. It looks and smells incredible.

She smiles, having recovered from my inappropriate question. "I love to cook. Especially breakfast foods. And yes, I can help you get cleaned up. I don't mind. We can do that after we eat. I'm starving."

Elyse and I eat breakfast and talk about normal things. Is this what it would have been like if Nicole was still alive? Would she have been able to get over the past? Would my sister and I sit down for Sunday brunch and talk like we used to? Elyse is slightly older, and definitely more of a people person than Nicole, but still, I can't help but feel a pang of sadness when I think of how she should be here with us right now. I don't think I will ever stop feeling that, no matter how much time passes.

"So, did you ask your hot friend to dinner on Tuesday? Garrett will be back early that evening, so it's still on."

I concentrate on the piece of egg I have just speared with

my fork. "Well, the thing is we kind of had a little disagreement."

Elyse gives me a knowing look. "Paige, I like to think I'm very good at reading people, so I apologize if this is out of line, but you seem to be the emotionally closed-off type. Right?"

I shrug. "I suppose that's true."

She nods. "So when you say disagreement, what you're really saying is that you are trying your best to keep him at an arm's length, yes?"

"I just can't afford to complicate my life right now, and he is a major complication."

Elyse throws her fork down on her plate. "He's not a complication, Paige. You are. Just relax and let things happen. Everyone needs people in their life. Everyone. Trust me, I have at least 10 more life experience years than you do."

"We'll see," I tell her.

We finish eating and I put our dishes in the machine.

"So, you're sure you don't mind the shower thing? I realize it's not entirely normal for me to ask, especially since I've just met you."

Elyse shakes her head. "Please, Paige. We're women. We help one another. That's just a fact of life."

Well, Elyse obviously did not have the same upbringing that I did. She probably came from a close, loving family. I

MIRIAM EPSTEIN

just nod in agreement, and we head towards my bathroom.

Chapter Sixteen

After I'm all cleaned up and Elyse has placed a fresh dressing over my arm, I walk her to the door.

"Thank you for everything today, Elyse. I really appreciate it."

Elyse looks down at the hardwood floors, as if they are incredibly fascinating. "No, thank you. I was really looking forward to spending time with Garrett this weekend, and if you hadn't been around, I would probably be feeling sorry for myself."

She squeezes my hand quickly, and then opens the door. To find Brady, standing there, hand poised to knock.

"Hello, I'm Elyse. Paige's neighbor."

Brady puts his hand out to shake hers. "Nice to meet you, Elyse. I'm Brady."

I am still standing statue-like behind Elyse.

She steps to the side and I can see a hint of mischief in her expression. "Brady, great. I'm glad I ran into you so that I can tell you we changed dinner time on Tuesday. My fiancee gets in around 6:30 from a trip, so I'd like to have both of you over at eight. See you then!"

That traitorous woman. She takes off down the hall and is inside her apartment lightening quick.

Brady turns to me. "Is it alright if I come in?"

I nod my head in the direction of the living room. "Sure."

Instead of the couch, Brady chooses the love seat and pulls me down with him so that I am practically sitting in his lap. He takes both of my hands in his and strokes my skin with his thumbs.

"I'm sorry. I don't want last night to mess up our friendship."

"It didn't, and it won't. You don't have anything to be sorry for. You have been nothing but nice to me since I met you. And I didn't really deserve your generosity, especially when I spilled coffee all over you."

He laughs. "I like you a lot, Paige, and I don't think this is one-sided. Is it?"

I have been unconsciously stroking my index finger back and forth over the black suede upholstery, creating that contrast of dark and light that used to annoy my mother when I did it back home. I see now why it bothered her; when things aren't in place, it can create chaos even in the mind of someone. If I choose to lie about my feelings for Brady, it may cost me in the form of someone that has made me smile for the first time in a long time. If I tell him the truth, it will almost certainly backfire at some point.

I cannot bring myself to lie about this, so I tell him the truth as succinctly as possible. "It is not one-sided."

He smiles. "We did just meet last week, though, and I practically forced my friendship upon you."

I can't help but grin. "Yes, that you did, but it's been a good thing."

"I'm glad you think so. I just want to tell you that I would like to continue to wear you down until you realize how awesome I am and throw yourself at me, but I'll let you do it at your own pace. Cool?"

The urge to hug him comes over me so suddenly that I don't think about what I'm doing until my arms are around him and I really am sitting in his lap. He pulls me to him even closer, and the pressure of his embrace is something I've needed for so very long. I bury my head in his shoulder and he strokes my hair down my back.

Too quickly, I realize this is absolutely the last thing I should be doing after the talk we just had. I stand up. When you have denied yourself a very basic human craving like the need for physical comfort for so very long, the first time you feel it again can be your undoing. There are few things in life better than feeling safe in someone's arms. And now that I've reawakened my need for that security, that closeness, I want it more. I very well may have opened Pandora's box.

"I just need to use the restroom. I'll be right back."

Brady nods and I dash off to my bedroom. I just need a moment to breathe; a moment to shake off the overwhelming urge to disregard everything he just said about taking things slowly. I turn on the tap and dampen a wash cloth with cool water. I run it over my forehead and cheeks, hoping it will cool me off and slow my heart rate. I look at myself very closely in the mirror that now scares me a little, since it bore my sister's name in lipstick the color of blood. I take notice of the color in my cheeks. The hollow underneath my eyes has a lot less purple. My lips, usually chapped from biting them anxiously and not using anything to moisturize, look smoother and plumper. I almost feel pretty again.

Feeling as though I've quieted the desire to throw myself at Brady, I turn the light off by the vanity and exit my bedroom. Walking down the hallway, I take note of how bare my walls are. The apartment looks barely lived in. Maybe it is time to add some of my personality to this place.

Brady is holding something in his hand; he is studying it so hard that he doesn't seem to hear me come back into the room. He doesn't look up until I sit back down next to him. I see that he is looking at a photograph.

He turns the picture so that I can see it. "You were a cute kid, Paige. Who is this in the picture with you, your sister? You look a lot like her."

FROM YESTERDAY

The color I noticed in my cheeks must be draining away as I stare at the picture. Yes, it is in fact me and Nicole. The picture was taken on the day of her Junior Prom, so she is about sixteen and I am thirteen. She is wearing her dress, a royal blue floor length strapless gown with a sweetheart neckline and crystal beading along the top. I am in plain jeans and a t-shirt, just there to wish my big sister a fun evening. I loved that picture of her so much, she looked so beautiful in her dress. I couldn't stop staring at that photo after Nicole died.

That picture was with the pile of my things taken from me on the day I entered Broad Horizons. It was never returned to me.

Chapter Seventeen

After what seems like hours, but is probably just a few minutes, I am able to close my eyes and win my desperate battle for air. Once my breathing is under control, I keep my eyes closed and listen. It is true that denying one of the five senses can strengthen the others; my hearing is sharper than ever right now.

A whimper, and then an angry shout. Those are from a female. Nicole. Followed shortly by a gruff male voice telling her to shut her mouth. Footsteps, and then a bottle clanking down on a hard surface. More footsteps, and finally, the chilling sound of my sister trying to scream behind something that muffles her voice.

Oh, god. He could be strangling her. Or smothering her.

And I am next.

When I hear the sound of a large object being dragged across the room, my fatalistic brain imagines the dead body of my sister as the one being dragged.

Don't be dead. Don't be dead. Don't be dead.

I repeat this in my head over and over until the closet door opens and light spills inside so heavily that I am momentarily blinded. As my eyes adjust, I see the hulking figure of Turner coming at me with a cloth in his hand. He puts it over my mouth.

Chloroform.

I struggle and try not to breathe, but I can only hold out for so long. There is no slow fade out from waking to sleep. No time to try and pull away. The chemical works instantly.

It is a while before I remember anything else.

Monday morning brings me a moment of peace and clarity. I drink my coffee outside, on the balcony. There are few things more enjoyable than the smell of newness that is brought from a hard rain. The sun isn't entirely present; gray storm clouds line half of the sky, but the rest of it is blue and welcoming.

Though I am troubled by the reappearance of a picture I did not bring to Florida from Ohio, I am happy to have it back. I will not even let myself start to wonder how it got here, I don't need the extra fuel on the fire to drive myself crazy. Brady even let it go after I confirmed that the girl in the picture with me was in fact my sister. He left it at that and didn't try to extract any additional details.

I don't talk about my dead sister, nor the circumstances surrounding her death, to anyone. No matter how attractive I may find him, he was not about to be the exception.

I throw on jeans and an Ohio State t-shirt, and toss a light sweater in my bag for the cold classrooms. The class I share with Brady, Diverse Populations, is my first of the day. Sometimes I wonder why an introvert such as myself chose Social Work as her major. It's not less than a little bit ironic.

Brady raises his eyebrows when I walk into class. "Ohio State, huh? Buckeyes fan?"

I shimmy my hips a little and wink. "And so what if I am?"

"I don't have a problem with it, I'm just curious as to why you are an OSU fan, I guess. I know FIU isn't really a major football team, yet, but why not UF or the U, or some other big Florida team?"

I shrug and pretend to dig through my bag for a pen so that I don't have to elaborate. Perhaps wearing this shirt wasn't the smartest thing I could have done.

Dr. Reyes arrives just then and Brady forgets all about the shirt while we listen to our instructions for today's class. It would appear that there is no lecture today, which is nice, but the in-class assignment is one that I think may cause me trouble.

"As students of Social Work, and especially where it pertains to diversity, your people skills have to be at the top of their game. You will need to be able to talk to anyone, no matter their background, and be able to connect with them on any level which will put them at ease. It is your job to obtain as much information as possible, all the while getting your subject to trust you. So, while this may seem a bit overdone, we will pair up today and interview one another. I'm providing each of you with a list of questions that should help get you started, but it will be up to you to use your quick thinking and dig just a little bit deeper. You have the entire 75 minutes to complete this assignment. Go ahead, pair up. Please try and choose someone you did not meet before this semester."

With that, the professor steps away from the lectern and sits behind the media desk. Brady and I immediately turn towards one another.

"Well, we did only just meet on the first day of classes, so we're good. Right, partner?"

I sigh in exaggerated frustration. "I suppose you'll do."

The stack of papers containing the questions reaches us a minute later and we each take one before passing the rest to the next row.

Brady turns his chair so that he faces me. "These are pretty straightforward, fairly boring questions. Do you want to start? Or maybe we can take turns. I ask you a question, then I answer the same one?"

I hate answering questions, but I nod anyway. "Yes, that will work. We can take turns, but I'll ask first. So, question one. What is your full name?"

"Brady Shae Quinlan. Yours?"

"Wow, so very Irish. I'm Paige Kerimov."

He frowns. "What about your middle name?"

"What about it? I don't have one."

"Everyone has a middle name."

"Apparently not everyone, because I do not. Next question. What is your date of birth?"

"October 27th, 1994."

"I'm May 6th, '95."

I pause before I ask him the third question. A minute ago I was avoiding telling him I'm from Ohio, but the very next question would bring that right back up. Should I tell him the truth? I don't want anyone to have enough information about me to be able to dig up skeletons best left buried, but if I start lying there is a very good chance of me slipping up. This, right here, is the very reason I don't let people get close. I don't like to lie.

"Paige? You still here?"

"Yes, sorry. Okay, where were you born?"

"Good old, Boston, Mass."

His accent comes on just a little too thick just then and I smirk. "That's wicked awesome, Brady."

He laughs. "I don't think I have said wicked once since I moved here. What about you? Wait, let me guess. Columbus, Ohio?"

So, the truth then. "Close. I'm from Cleveland. Where

were your parents born?"

"Both of them were born and raised in Boston. It is my grandfather that came here from Northern Ireland."

"My parents came here from the Ukraine. We're Russian."

"I gathered, the last name and all."

I choose to the ignore the sarcasm in his voice. We go through another ten minutes of mundane questions before things start getting a bit more personal. It's not asking for deep, dark, secrets, but it becomes less about your first pet's name and more about who you are as a person. And then, at the very end, does my discomfort really take over.

The last question is an instruction to both partners to take things further and ask the questions that will really tell you who your partner is.

I try not to ask anything too personal of Brady when we start that section, in the hopes that if I go easy on him then he will do the same. "Was FIU your first choice? Where else did you apply?"

Brady doesn't take any time to answer. "Yes, actually, it was my first choice. I wanted to be in South Florida near the beach and in the warm weather. The Social Work program here is very highly rated, as I'm sure you know. I also applied at some California schools, and Boston University."

I look up. "BU? Why? You said you wanted to be in the warm weather."

"I know, but I didn't want my father to think I was trying to get away from him. I wasn't. I just needed a change of scenery. I didn't get in to BU, but I wouldn't have gone there even if I had."

I can't think of anything else to say.

"So, Paige, I think you have exceeded your one question per turn, yes? I'll be taking full advantage of that right now."

He smirks.

"Of course you will, Brady."

"Tell me about your sister."

My heart stops beating for a moment, I could almost swear it. "What, uh, what are you talking about?"

"The girl in the picture yesterday. She has to be related to you. Older sister, I'm sure. Tell me about her."

I look down at my paper, trying to keep my panic at bay. "There's not much to tell. She's dead."

My words don't have the intended effect. Most people would grow uncomfortable in this situation, or offer empty condolences. When I glance back up, Brady is watching me with expectation, waiting for more. When I don't continue, he prods me, albeit gently.

"People die, Paige. Believe me, I know. But we should celebrate who these people were to us. Tell me who she was to you."

"Fine. People always talk about the deceased as if they were saints. My sister was not. Nicole was smart, and daring. She was confident. I envied that confidence, but I was a shy little kid. Nicole did her best to break me out of my shell, even if it meant she had to get me in trouble to do so. She wasn't kind, and she wasn't generous. But she took care of me; she let me tag along with her like the annoying little sister that I was. I loved her. And then she killed herself."

I stand up, grab my things, and take off before Brady has a chance to process.

chapter eighteen

A growing sense of dread takes over my stomach as I make my way towards Elyse's apartment on Tuesday evening. Three times I nearly convinced myself that it wouldn't be *that* bad if I made up some excuse not to go. I could say that I was sick, or that I fell down the stairs and broke my big toe, or something else equally lame. Of course, I quickly realized that when you live in the same building with the only two people in the world that are guaranteed to come over and check on you, those lies will catch up to you. So, here I am about to knock on the door with a nice bottle of wine, courtesy of Nicole's fake Ohio driver's license. The fact that it is an Ohio I.D. is probably the only reason I get away with it; most Floridians only know the things to look for in a fraudulent Florida license.

I'm fifteen minutes early on purpose. Showing up at the same time as Brady would give Elyse the wrong impression and I don't need to encourage her unfortunate matchmaking desires.

FROM YESTERDAY

"Hi, Paige! Oh, thank you! This is a really great Cabernet."

Elyse answers the door and I already want to kick myself when I see her in a dressy green wrap dress and heels. Her makeup looks professional; trendy cat eyeliner and deep red lips done properly. I am wearing jeans that are worn and frayed at the bottom, and a t-shirt that says "Support Animal Rights: Sleep with a Vegetarian". The only makeup I have on is some vanilla-flavored lip balm.

And then it gets worse.

I may be a few minutes early, but Brady managed to beat me here anyway. His social etiquette apparently far better than mine, he has on nice jeans and an untucked button down shirt in the same color of blue as his eyes. I can't help but stare at him for a moment, until we make eye contact and I force myself to look away before *he* sees too much of *me*.

"Hi."

He breaks the silence first, like I knew he would. He speaks softly, probably afraid I'll run away if he raises his voice any louder than a whisper.

"I'm sorry."

It just comes out before I can stop myself. I look down at the floor. I was a bitch yesterday and the guilt I feel is suffocating. I look back and see Elyse is in the kitchen and out of earshot. Good. This is a private moment between me and Brady; one I probably should have tried to do before we arrived.

He pulls me to him for a brief hug. "Don't be sorry, Paige. We're okay."

When he lets go of me, I look up at him again. Nothing more needs to be said and there is something so incredible about a friendship like that. Other than Nicole, I have never known what that was like before now.

The sound of a key turning in the lock breaks the spell and Elyse comes rushing out of the kitchen to greet Garrett. It's a little too June and Ward Cleaver, but kind of nice at the same time. I feel like a voyeur as I watch them kiss; Garrett even tips her backwards. Brady and I exchange a look in which I see mirth in his eyes. I suppress my own smile.

Eventually, Elyse and Garrett remember that they are not alone and they come into the living room to join us.

Elyse introduces Garrett to Brady and they shake hands.

"And you remember Paige, right?"

He smiles at me. "Of course. We met just the other day. And Elyse talks about you non-stop. If you weren't a woman, I might even be jealous!"

I laugh, though a bit uncomfortably. Garrett seems almost too nice and polite.

Elyse, who had slipped back into the kitchen during to introductions, comes back out with the bottle of wine I brought over and four glasses. "Dinner is ready, everyone. Let's all sit at the table."

FROM YESTERDAY

The dining room table seats six; two of the places at either end of the table. Garrett sits at one end, Elyse to his right, I'm on his left, and Brady is next to me. Garrett opens the bottle of wine and pours some for each of us. When he reaches me, he pauses.

"I'm not sure I should be serving you alcohol, Paige. You're only nineteen, right?"

I don't say anything. I couldn't care less about the wine. I just don't like being the center of attention, which I am at the moment.

After a few seconds that seem to stretch on forever, Garrett laughs and pours some wine into my glass. "I'm kidding. I'm not policing anyone's choices here. Besides, you brought this. It would be pretty rude to deny you, right?"

I smile. I know he's just trying to be a charming host. Still, Brady catches my eye and kind of rolls his eyes in solidarity. It instantly makes me feel more at ease. I reach over and squeeze his hand under the table, thanking him. When I pull my hand back, I let the tips of my fingers linger in his palm for a moment.

Elyse starts serving the meal. She has made enough food for the SFU football team. There are more serving dishes than there is room on the table, with some of it having to stay on the breakfast bar.

"How did you two meet?" Garrett asks as he slices his chicken into neat squares.

"Paige crashed into me, quite literally. On the first day of the semester."

We all laugh.

"I wasn't paying attention to where I was going. And then Brady practically forced me to partner up for our semester project."

Garrett looks amused. "And what are your majors? Are you both in the same program?"

I let Brady answer Garrett's questions. "We are in the same program. Social Work. Although I'm a Junior and Paige is a Sophomore, so this one course is the only one we have together right now."

The men continue to make small talk and Elyse interjects every once in a while. She seems content to simply gaze adoringly at Garrett for the most part. I only answer questions when asked directly, which is seldom. I don't feel bad about being so quiet, though, because Brady and Garrett have moved on to football talk and they are very animated about it. Finally, everyone is finished eating and I get up to help Elyse clear the dishes.

"Oh, no, Paige. Please sit. You're my guest."

"It's no big deal, Elyse. I want to help."

Garrett puts a hand on her arm. "Love, while I would never suggest that dishes are a woman's job, if you and Paige want to take care of it, Brady and I can set up for some more drinks on the balcony until you join us."

It's his insincerity, I notice right then. Everything he does *is* over the top; almost to the point of being disingenuous. I shrug it off because I have a habit of being naturally suspicious of anyone's motives. Plus, he seems to love Elyse as much as she loves him, even if he does expect her to wait on him hand and foot. Brady tosses me a look over his shoulder as the guys retreat to the balcony.

I stack a few plates on my arms, waitress-style, and follow Elyse into the kitchen.

"I'm so glad you two could make it tonight, Paige. It's tough being here alone so often. Garrett travels for work at least a two times every month, sometimes more."

I take the dishes she has already rinsed and load them into the dishwasher. "I am sure that is incredibly lonely. Miami isn't exactly a mecca for friendly faces, either."

"That's very true. I grew up in a small town and I knew everyone. It wasn't until college that I got to see what it was like having some anonymity. As much as I enjoy having my privacy, the small town girl in me really misses having a large extended family nearby."

I cannot relate, for obvious reasons, but I fake it to the best of my abilities. "I get it. It's nice to have a built-in support system if you are used to that. I suppose I just love my independence. That's why I chose such a large school."

Elyse nods. "One of the first things I noticed about you

was that you tend to be a bit... well... separate. You like to keep your distance from everything around you. I guess I'm just a bit too pushy, and I hope I didn't make you uncomfortable when I practically forced my friendship upon you."

"Actually, I may have been resistant initially, but I'm glad you are here. I've been warming up to the idea of having someone to talk to other than myself lately."

I put the last of the dishes into the washer as Elyse dries the last pot. "Thanks for the help with this, Paige. Let's go join the guys outside."

She grabs my hand and we walk out to the sliding glass door off of the living room. One of my favorite features of this building is the size of the balconies. There is enough room on the main balcony for each unit to house a table and chairs and various other items. The second balcony off of the master bedroom is smaller, but still quite spacious. Because Elyse lives in an end unit, her apartment has a view of Oleta river and the ocean. At night, with all of the city lights, it is absolutely breathtaking. I settle into the seat next to Brady as Elyse sits on the lip on the chair Garrett is in. A bottle of scotch and two tumblers sit half full on the table.

Garrett reaches for his glass. "Would you like a drink, Paige?"

"No, thank you. I'm pretty set from the wine we had."

"Brady and I were just talking about his life in Boston. He

says you are from Ohio. I have some family there, about an hour or so away from Cleveland, in Mansfield."

I give Brady the side-eye. He is impassive. "Oh, yes. I've been there. It's a nice little town."

Garrett laughs. "No, it's not. It is boring as can be, but it's nice of you to pretend otherwise. Is your family still in Cleveland, or did you move here with them?"

I shift in my seat. "They are still in Ohio."

"You must miss them very much, then. It isn't easy being away from home."

Garrett glances meaningfully at Elyse when he says this, but his gaze holds more annoyance than compassion.

"I've adjusted pretty well. Listen, I hate to take off so early, but I have a morning class. Thank you so much for dinner."

Elyse looks disappointed, and Garrett is a bit put off. "That's a shame, but we certainly remember what it was like to hit those eight AM courses."

Garrett laughs. "Maybe you do, Love, but I learned my lesson after my first semester not to schedule a course before noon."

Brady gets up. "Well, I would agree with you, but not all the courses are offered at various times here. Paige's early class is the one we share, so I think I'll head out as well. It was a pleasure meeting you both. Thanks again for an amazing meal."

Brady places a hand at the small of my back to guide me off of the balcony and into the living room. "I'll walk you home."

I wait until we are in the hallway before I respond. "I live right there. I think I'll manage."

"Yeah, but you've been drinking. Wouldn't want you to get lost. And I should come in and check for sharp corners you could hit yourself on."

I poke a finger into this chest as we reach my door. "I had a glass of wine. You, my friend, are the one who has been drinking. How much scotch did you have, anyway? You sound a bit slurred."

"Nah, I'm just barely tipsy. I'm good. You're right, though. Tonight is definitely not the night for me to be alone with you in your apartment. Goodnight, Paige."

He leaves me standing there with my mouth gaping slightly. I don't have to be a genius to figure out what he meant. Sighing, I unlock my front door and step inside.

And then I stop moving; stop breathing.

The floor in my apartment, all of it, is covered in dead sterling roses.

The sterling rose was Nicole's favorite. It was the flower we used when we buried her.

chapter nineteen

I cannot pretend that I'm imagining this stuff any longer. I'm forced to admit this as I sweep up the dead flowers and toss them into a garbage bag. Three garbage bags full, actually, by the time I finish. I take everything to the trash room and chuck it through the chute as quickly as possible.

When I get back to my unit, I pause in the hall before going back inside. Brady is downstairs. I don't want to be alone. I could just...

No.

I don't need to be a poor little distressed girl and throw myself at someone who had the self-control to back off when he knew he'd had too much to drink. I'd be playing with fire, and in my heightened emotional state, I would either say too much or sleep with him and ruin our friendship.

I go inside.

My cell phone has almost no battery left, so I connect it to the wall charger and pick up the land line. I hit the asterisk key, then six and seven before dialing an all to familiar number. It rings three times before a heavily accented male voice comes on the line. "Yah."

I try not to breathe.

"Hello? Someone is there? Hello?"

I hang up and stare at the phone. It is painful to hear my father's voice and not beg him for forgiveness. Or scream at him to beg for mine, because I am still waiting for an apology from both my parents. But we are not there yet, not one of us. Too much Russian pride.

The question I really have to ask myself is why I should feel the least bit of comfort from hearing the voice of a man who condemned me rot in that hospital room? Why do I call the people that I have worked so very hard to keep from finding out where I am for so long? I have done this to hear my mother's voice before, too. I don't know how these things work, but I'm sure if they really wanted to, my parents could trace the calls even though I blocked them. Technology is far too advanced for me to believe otherwise.

Yet, they haven't tried. I'm sure they know who is on the other line.

I could be totally off, though. Even with all the financial resources my parents have, maybe tracing a call like that is only available to the police or something. Still, they could absolutely have hired someone to look for me. It's not like I haven't left little clues here and there, whether I meant to or not.

The truth is, as tough as I pretend to be, I don't think I'll ever be able to completely forget about what it's like to feel safe and secure in my parent's arms. It's a childish impulse, but there have been days where all I wanted was to cry to my mother and ask her to take my pain away.

Not that she would ever be able to. Especially not with all the hurt my sister and I have caused her in the last few years.

I push this futile conversation I'm having with myself out of my head What matters right now is figuring out why someone is sneaking into my home, in a building with security that the secret service would approve of, and leaving me little "gifts" that I suspect are meant to scare the hell out of me, which is a success so far, because the next thing I do is to go grab my gun and make sure it is loaded. I keep it with me in the bathroom as I shower, setting it down where I can see it from the tub. After I've put on a t-shirt and shorts to sleep in, I set it on the nightstand next to me, making sure to aim the gun towards the balcony and not at the wall where an unsuspecting neighbor might be sleeping in case of accidental discharge.

The gun is the only reason I am able to sleep at all.

Chapter Twenty

Between the stressful evening I had and the shallow sleep, it's no surprising that I look terrible this morning. And of course the first person that I'll see when I get to class is Brady. Rather, the only person that I'll care about seeing, anyway.

I spend a little extra time getting ready, especially on the makeup since I can use concealer to look less strung out. I even shave my legs and put a cute little sun dress on, and it isn't even black. This shade of lilac makes my hazel eyes appear just a little bit brighter and my gloss makes my lips look a bit fuller. I'm good to go.

The weather has been cooling off considerably for late September. I didn't expect that until early November, but I can't say that I mind. It's nice enough, and I plenty of time so I walk to campus. By the time I get there, my mood has improved and I think I'll be able to avoid scrutiny from a certain overly perceptive friend.

As I turns out, I'm wrong.

FROM YESTERDAY

"Man, I feel like I got run over."

These are Brady's first words to me when he stumbles into class a few minutes after me.

"I guess you shouldn't have had that last glass of scotch, huh?"

He looks at me with half-slit eyes. "You look like you drank a bit too much yourself. No, actually, I take that back. You look as great as always, but you put effort into it. Suspicious effort."

"Shut up."

Okay, not a great comeback by far, but class begins and he can't say anything back during the lecture. And it is a long lecture. Dr. Reyes is one of those professors that teaches with great enjoyment, but he goes off on tangents and spends 20 minutes on one section. And even though this is my major, it's not always very interesting material.

After class, I wait for Brady instead of darting off as quickly as I can. He wouldn't have been able to catch up with me today; I've seen molasses move faster than Brady with a hangover.

"Need me to carry your books for you, Lush?" I quip.

He gives me the fakest laugh I have ever heard, then immediately scowls at me. "You're funny. And no thank you. I would love it if you would teach my Spinning class for me later, though."

I wince in sympathy. "Oh, wow. That's going to really suck for you."

He nods. "Yes, it is. I'm just lucky I have several hours to sleep it off before then. And a really good friend who is going to take the class and lend me moral support."

He swats my butt.

"Yes, so long as you leave my butt alone."

"Okay, but it's a really nice-"

"Brady."

He holds his hands up in surrender. "Sorry. No ass slapping. See you at five?"

"I'll be there."

He turns to the parking lot, then pauses and flips around back to me. "Is your arm okay? Have you been taking the antibiotic?"

"Yes," I say. "Why?"

"Don't take this the wrong way because you look beautiful, you always do, but you also look stressed. And a little bit upset. I thought maybe your arm was bothering you."

I wave my hand. "No, I just didn't sleep enough. I'm good. Get some rest."

We go our separate ways.

Why is it getting so hard to lie to him? I had a moment there where I desperately wanted to tell him everything about me, about my sister, about the strange things that have been happening lately. It's selfish, though. It would be nothing more than an unburdening for me; for him it would serve no purpose other than admitting to him that he made a huge mistake befriending me. These past few weeks are evidence that trouble follows me, no matter how far I try to run.

Chapter Twenty-one

"That was impressive, Brady. You barely looked hungover at all during the whole class."

Brady passes me a water bottle as the rest of the students file out of the little cycling classroom. Dehydrated from the intense exercise, I drink the whole thing down in one shot. Brady looks impressed.

"Wow. You're thirsty. That was an entire liter of water."

"Yes, thanks. It was nice and cold."

I wink at him and then pick up my bag. I get to the door before I notice he's not following me. Turning around, I catch him staring at me in the mirror. "Are you coming, or are you just going to stand there and stare at my ass?"

Brady's mouth opens for a second; I obviously caught him off guard. Finally, he shrugs and starts to walk. "Sorry, Paige. I'm usually better at that."

"Better at what?"

"Better at not getting caught staring at your ass."

I toss the empty water bottle at him, but he catches it. "Obviously some of your reflexes are still intact."

"I'm not completely useless. You still up for getting some work done? We can work on he project at my place. I'll order pizza."

I think about it for a moment. The right thing to do for Brady would be to cut this friendship off now, while I can still manage to save *some* hurt feelings. I'm a danger to him; I firmly believe that.

But I can't. I would miss him too much. How selfish am I?

Very, as it turns out. "Yes, that's perfect. I'll just run home and shower first. You're on the twenty-second floor, right?"

He nods. "Yes, unit 2205. I'll leave the door unlocked for you. Just come in when you're ready."

I wave to him and go to the women's locker room. There are very few students in the gym today; not one other girl in the locker room. It is eerily quiet.

I get my things as quickly as I can. Just as I'm about to go, a locker door slams shut in one of the other rows.

Strange. No one was in here, and I didn't hear anyone else come in. I start to peek around the corner to see if anyone is there when another locker door is slammed. Startled, I drop my keys and the sound echoes loudly throughout the room.

I don't believe I am alone in here after all. It would be

wise for me to get out of here as quickly as I can. I get my keys from the floor and run out of the locker room with lightening speed, but not before I hear one more locker door slammed.

When I get to my car, I thank my running late earlier for forcing me to drive back to campus this afternoon. I want to be as far from here as possible right now. I drive fast enough to make it home in less than two minutes. I don't even care if I get stopped by campus police; a ticket would be preferable over whatever, or whomever, was back at that gym.

After parking my car in the garage, I enter the lobby of the building and I am comforted by the familiar sight of two security guards at the front desk, and all the other measures in place to keep unwanted visitors out of here.

That's when I remember that whoever this is has already been inside my apartment.

Chapter Twenty-Two

I take a shower quickly, dress in a skirt made of terry-cloth material and a tank top, and haul ass down to Brady's place. Being alone in my apartment sounds less and less appealing. Guns are not allowed on campus even with a concealed weapons permit, so I have had it locked up at home all day and I leave it there. I don't know if Brady would be bothered by having a gun in his house and I am not in the mood to get on the subject of why I have one. He still doesn't know that the gun he saw that day was mine.

I knock lightly on Brady's door before opening it, just in case. After all, you never know when you are going to walk into someone's home and see them standing by the refrigerator, drinking a glass of water and wearing nothing but a towel.

His skin is dry, but his hair hangs down in damp waves. Muscle defines every inch of his body. And I can see it all, well, most of it. The slightly wet towel tied around his waist is clingy and the outline of his perfectly shaped behind is mesmerizing. The towel ends at mid thigh, and as Brady slowly turns in my direction, I discover that things are being outlined that leave little to the imagination. I should be the one drinking water because my mouth is suddenly dry.

"I'm sorry!"

I blurt out the apology, but I can't seem to make myself turn away. So now I've walked in on him, been caught staring, and continue to embarrass myself.

Brady laughs. "What are you sorry for, Paige? I told you to just come in. If I minded you seeing me in a towel, I probably wouldn't be in the kitchen wearing only that."

"So, you did that on purpose?"

He grins. "Maybe. Maybe not. Let's say it wasn't a conscious decision, but you know how those pesky subconscious decisions can arise."

"Your subconscious wanted me to see you half naked? Uh, sure."

"Maybe I just wanted to see your reaction. Which was priceless, by the way. I'll go get dressed. Make yourself comfortable."

I take in the room while I wait for him. This is a one bedroom unit, other than that the layout is nearly identical to mine. His furniture is a set I recognize from an Ikea catalog; dark wood with very clean lines. A futon is the only seating in the living room, and it faces the wall which is dominated by a massive flat screen television. Underneath the TV is a low to the ground entertainment unit with stereo equipment and a video game console.

I sit at the breakfast bar and take out my binder with my notes for our project. I've done all of my part of the research; if Brady has completed his then all we have to do is type everything up and create some kind of visual presentation.

"Would you like something to drink?"

I nearly jump off of the barstool. I didn't hear him return.

"Uh, just some water, please."

"Why are you so nervous, Paige?"

He winks, the bastard. He knows why I'm on edge, or at least he knows what his part in my anxiety is. All of the other stuff isn't his fault at all. I give him the finger. He cracks up.

"Wow, that is not a gesture I'd ever guess you would make. I like it."

"What do you mean? Why wouldn't I make a rude gesture?"

Brady looks sheepish now. "Because you're just... kind of perfect."

I don't say anything, not right away. Silence hangs in the air, not in an awkward way, but with a modicum of emotion that touches me and energizes him.

I break the spell. "I'm as far from perfect as I possibly

could be, Brady, and I'm sorry because inevitably you will see why."

"I don't believe you. You just don't see yourself for who you really are. Most people don't."

I purse my lips and turn my head to the side to avoid the intensity with which he focuses on me. He doesn't let me escape, though. He reaches for me and tips my face back towards him and leans in. All the way in.

We stare at one another for a microsecond before I feel his lips on my own. They linger lightly at first, and then a simple touch becomes a kiss as he presses forward with intensity. Our mouths dance together as we each test the waters; a gentle bite, a tiny slip of tongue, each one of us seeking to match the rhythm of the other. His hand snakes up the back of my neck until it is in my hair, bringing me even closer to him. I'm between his thighs, nearly falling off the edge of the barstool. The kiss becomes open-mouthed and we taste one another; I take hold of his t-shirt with both hands and breathe him in through my nose. His scent is warm and masculine and I'm drugged by it. I want to be.

Until I don't anymore.

Reality is a harsh slap in the face when I come to my senses and remember who I am. I let go of his shirt, place my hands on his upper arms, and push him away from me until I have space to stand up. He looks up, still blissfully unaware of what I'm about to do.

FROM YESTERDAY

"You're amazing," he tells me.

I shake my head and back away. "I'm wrong, all wrong. I'll ruin you. Please, I can't."

And then I'm running out the door; always running away from any possibility of a good thing because if there is one thing that I am certain of, it is that any happiness I may have comes with an expiration date.

Chapter Twenty-Three

I know something is off the moment I walk through my door. There is a heaviness in the air that I didn't feel before I left, but I did feel it every time some fucked up little gift has been left for me in the past few weeks. Now I wish I'd taken the Glock with me when I went downstairs.

I take a deep breath and go further into the apartment, hoping I can get to my gun if someone is still here. I don't think there is, though; I feel as though I'm alone.

The vase, the Swarovski crystal vase that I loved enough to bring with me, it is no longer on the end table by the love seat. Instead, it is now a jigsaw puzzle that I will never be able to solve. Millions of little pieces lay scattered throughout the living and dining rooms, and there is some dark substance coating much of it. I get closer, careful not to step on any shards that will cut through my thin ballet flats.

My hand flies to my mouth and I suppress the urge to vomit. The dark stuff? It is blood. Wet, sticky blood.

I'm kneeling on the floor next to this mess of a life that belongs to me, frozen in place, when the front door flies open.

"Are you kidding me, Paige? Really? You're so damn infuriating. I thought we were finally over this up and down bullshit!"

Brady is yelling, but it is the most comforting sound I could possibly hope to hear in this moment. And then I see him in my peripheral vision.

"What the... is that your blood? Paige, are you okay?"

He rushes over to me, grabs me by the arms, and lifts me up to check me over.

"It's not mine."

"Whose is it then? What is going on?"

Now he is practically shaking me.

"It's time for you to start talking, Paige. Is someone bothering you? Should I call the police."

Mentioning the cops snaps me back to reality and I look up at him; fear is prevalent in all my features. "No! No police. You can't."

Brady lets go of me and crosses his arms over his chest. "Fine, but tell me why."

I nod. "Okay. But I can't be in this room. Please, let's go into my spare bedroom."

I don't wait for him, nor do I look back to see if he's even moved from the spot he was standing in. I just go into the office and open the top drawer of my desk. This is where I'm keeping the lock box with my gun.

I sit down in my desk chair, take the gun out, and place it on the desk in plain view of Brady, who has just come in the room.

He walks around the desk to where I'm sitting and leans against it. "So, that gun was yours."

"Yes."

"A lot of strange things have been going on with you lately, Paige, but I think I'm starting to put two and two together. Will you please tell me the whole story?"

"I can only tell you what I know, which isn't a whole lot. I don't know the reason why someone is doing this stuff to me, but I also cannot lie about it any longer. And I have been keeping things from you."

Brady shrugs. "I know, Paige. I've been trying to be as patient as possible, but I'm really worried about you. I can't just keep my mouth shut any longer."

"I didn't want to involve you in this messed up life of mine. I tried to keep you from it, but after a while I didn't want to push you away anymore."

"You don't have to hide this. You need help, or at least someone to talk to. I want to be that person for you."

"Look, I don't know who has been sending me the

messages and breaking into my apartment. I really don't. If I believed in ghosts, and I absolutely do not, I'd think it was my dead sister doing this. Which is why this is even more fucked up, because they want me to think it is Nicole. Or they want me to be reminded of her unfortunate legacy."

Brady looks even more unsettled than he did a moment ago. "What happened to your sister, Paige?"

I close my eyes for a moment as I relive the pain of her death all over again.

"I don't. I mean, I can't. It is just too much. I wanted you to know that I am not okay; that someone is trying to scare me. And it probably has everything to do with what happened to my sister, but that story is not yet ready to be told. I'm sorry, but I need you to just give me more time. Can you do that?"

Brady reaches out and takes one of my hands in his. "Yes, Paige, I can do that. But that doesn't mean I can ignore the fact that you have, for all intents and purposes, a stalker."

This makes me shudder. I hadn't thought of it that way. He's right, though. All of this does kind of fall under the category of stalking. "I don't know what to do. I can't call the police. I have to figure this out by myself."

"You're not on your own, remember? We will figure this out. Starting with your safety. You shouldn't be spending time alone anymore."

I point to the gun. "I have protection with that. I'm an excellent shot. And you can't be with me all the time. I don't want a baby sitter."

"You can't take the gun with you to campus, so at least let me be with you to and from school. And even with a gun, you could be surprised and lose the advantage. I'm not trying to be a baby sitter, believe me, but I will do what I have to help you get out of this situation."

"The gun doesn't bother you?" I ask.

"No, I grew up around guns. My father taught me. He has a rather large collection of semi-automatic handguns and rifles. I have a .45 downstairs, but I haven't yet applied for my concealed carry license in Florida."

Brady puts the hand he's holding down onto my knee, but he doesn't let go. I don't say anything, I just look at his fingers intertwined with my own.

"One more thing, Paige. You need someone with a background in criminal justice to do a little research for you. Neither one of us is qualified for that, but I know someone who is."

I shake my head vigorously, keeping my focus on his hand "No cops, Brady."

"No, I promise. I'm talking about Victor. He's the daytime security guard at the front desk. He's a cool guy; we've played basketball a few times. He told me about the freelance private investigating he does. His brother runs a P.I. firm in the Gables. Those guys know how to be discreet."

"Okay, I'm fine with that."

All of a sudden the enormity of everything hits me hard. I feel weighed down and I slump forward a little bit on my chair. Brady catches me by the shoulders and pulls me towards him. I rest my cheek against his abdomen and his arms go around me as best as they can while he is standing and I am sitting. The expansion and contraction of his diaphragm as he breathes is a comfort to me; it soothes my anxiousness until my eyes are half-lidded and my inhibitions are fading. I reach my arms up and slide my hands down the front of his shirt until I am touching him just inside his hips. He sucks in a breath and pulls me up out of the chair, flips us around so that he is now the one sitting, and settles me in his lap to face him. I don't bother pulling my skirt down; I don't even think about the fact that I'm not wearing panties.

His cock is hard and I can feel him through the fabric of his cargo shorts against my bare, aching core. I lean forward, lick my lips slowly, and then gently bite down on his bottom lip. The shift forward means that my pubic bone feels the pressure of his erection and it is so damn good. He holds me there, pressing his lips to my own and deepening the kiss. I let myself rub against him just enough to make me crave him inside of me.

His hands roam down my back until he is gripping my hips and pulling me into him harder; grinding up against me as I push back down. The friction is intense and I am losing my ability to think straight.

I pull back from Brady's mouth, breaking the kiss and just moving against him; enjoying the sensation of muscles clenching. One of his hands leaves my hip and makes its way to the inside of my thigh, inching upward until I feel a soft touch just above my clit.

I groan, loudly and unapologetically; anticipating his next movement.

"Fuck, you aren't wearing any underwear, Paige."

I wriggle my hips and his finger has no choice but to move with me. "I know," I tell him, "less getting in the way."

My voice is hoarse and rough with lust; I barely even sound like me.

"God, you're amazing."

He doesn't sound any more in control of himself than I do. We continue the slow, heady grind against one another; seeking comfort, or release. Maybe both.

Then Brady pulls me up off of him and sets me on top of the desk. "I want to watch you make yourself come, Paige."

I don't question it. I'm too far gone by now. I just delve down and sink two fingers inside myself; my other hand goes to massage my clit.

It is unfathomable how much of a turn on it is to touch myself for him.

Brady watches, his hand gravitating towards the button of his shorts until he has them open and his erection is in his hand. I alternate between throwing my head back in ecstatic agony and glimpsing his hand work over his thick cock. Moisture is visible at the tip; a fact which pleases me because I know I've caused that. I press harder on my clit, then take my hand away briefly to raise my tank top over my head and bare my breasts to him. My nipples are sensitive to the cold air and it makes me shiver. I pull my fingers out of myself about halfway until I can see moisture coating them, and then thrust them back inside, causing me to cry out.

Brady strokes himself faster now, his breath coming in shallow gasps; he seems to swell up more in his hand. "You first," he tells me.

Knowing myself very well and exactly what to do to get where he wants me, it won't be long. I fuck myself with my fingers and rub my clit furiously with the other hand. And then the pressure becomes unbearable and I'm tipping over the edge. Falling, falling, falling until I hit the bottom and I let myself relax.

"Ah, Paige, I..."

As he starts to come, I lean forward so that he hits my breasts with every drop of his release. The extra visual is known to prolong an orgasm.

When we're both fully sated, I lean all the way back to lay down on my desk, not caring about the stickiness covering my chest. I bring my legs up to rest in his lap and he strokes the back of my calves gently.

"You are indescribable, Paige. I mean, I have no words."

I raise myself up onto my elbows to look at him. I don't speak, I just watch him as he gains control of his breathing and looks back at me.

After some time, I reach for the box of tissues on top of my filing cabinet and clean myself off. Brady takes them from me and tosses them into the wastebasket, then tucks himself back in and buttons his shorts. He picks my legs up as he stands, and lifts me into his arms so that I have to wrap my legs around his waist.

"Let's go to bed, Paige. I mean, to sleep."

I lay my head down on his chest and let him carry me into my bedroom. He sets me down on my bed, gently, and takes his clothing off. Standing before me completely nude, I cannot help but stare. I don't agree with anyone who says men aren't as nice to look at as women; I think that they are every bit as alluring. He is in great shape; muscle lines almost every surface. His cock is still semi-hard and hangs heavily between cut thighs.

He lets me admire him for a moment, then turns the light out and gets into the bed with me. I pull my skirt off to even the playing field and lay back as he raises the blanket over us both.

I flip so that I face away from him and lean back until I'm against his chest. One of Brady's arms comes to rest over my hip. He kisses the back of my neck.

FROM YESTERDAY

"Sleep well, Paige."

chapter Twenty-four

I'm awake long before Brady in the morning. I don't get up right away; I spend a few minutes enjoying the feeling of a warm body next to me and one of the most restful nights of sleep I've had in a long time. Eventually, I have to get up and use the bathroom and brush my teeth. I don't bother to get dressed; I just cover myself with a thin red robe. I look through my vanity for the extra toothbrush and leave it on the counter for Brady. I always buy a few because I'm paranoid about dropping mine and being unable to clean my mouth, so this one is new and in the package.

After making coffee, I check back in on Brady and he's still out. I'll bet he could sleep through a hurricane; my coffee maker is not a quiet machine. I grab my cell phone from my purse and step out onto the balcony for some privacy.

Dr. Sullivan answers on the second ring.

"Hey, Kid. I'm glad you called. I have something to tell you."

FROM YESTERDAY

If I don't tell her the truth right away, I'll lose my nerve, so I ignore what she's saying and jump right in. "It's happening again, Dr. Sullivan. I'm sure. He left me her necklace! The one we buried her with. I'm not making it up. He broke her vase; the one she begged my mother to get her for months. He left the shattered pieces all over my apartment floor with what looks like drops of blood on the broken pieces."

The silence on the other end of the phone lasts a bit too long. Finally, I hear her take a deep breath, probably preparing to tell me something she knows I won't want to hear.

I'm right. "Kiddo, listen to me. I want you to go and talk to someone local.

"Why? So that someone new can think that I'm crazy? No thanks. I'll talk to you and that's all."

"No one thinks you are crazy."

Anger starts to surge up inside of me. "You and I both know that's not the truth. What about my parents?"

She sighs. "Look, about your parents. Your father came to see me the other day."

The world stops spinning on its axis right then. "Did you tell him that you've spoken to me?"

"No, of course not. That's private information between me and you. He's still angry with me for letting you leave. He demanded I tell him where you are."

I breathe a little easier. "Well, that's another good reason for me not to tell you. He can't buy it out of you if you don't even know."

"I'd like to think that you trust me enough to know I would never succumb to a bribe, Kid."

"I know. I'm sorry. Look, I have to go. I'll call you again when I can."

"Wait, Rebecca..."

I hang up before she can say anything else and go back inside, careful not to step on any of the broken glass that I didn't bother to clean up last night. By the time I take a seat at the breakfast bar with my second cup of coffee, Brady finally makes an appearance. Unlike me, he opted out of covering himself up. Not that I mind, because he's definitely nice to look at, but it's hard to look anywhere else other than the obvious.

"Morning, Paige. Thanks for the toothbrush. Minty fresh."

He smirks. I roll my eyes.

"Well. You seem quite comfortable around me, huh? I'll bet you spend a lot of naked time when you're at your own place."

He nods as he takes a seat on the stool next to me."Absolutely, I do. Why not? I see no shame in being natural. And you saw everything last night, so why should I hide? You'll just spend all your time picturing me nude anyway."

I laugh. "You're too much. Do you want some coffee?"

"The answer to that question is always, always yes. Please."

I get up, and as I'm walking past him, he reaches out and lifts one side of my robe so that my ass is exposed. I smack his hand away.

"Just checking. You could take that off, you know."

"I could," I tell him, "but I think I like having you try to picture me naked."

I bring him his coffee and slide some sweetener in his direction.

"Oh, Paige. The images, they are burned into my mind. That still won't stop me from always wanting you to take your clothes off, though."

He takes a sip of his coffee and sighs contentedly. "Okay, now I can function properly. Which begs the question, should we fool around a little more and then call Victor, or vice versa?"

"That's a really tough decision to make, Brady. I mean, the responsible thing to do would be to call the guy and try to fix this problem, but on the other hand..."

I let my sentence trail off as I untie the sash around my waist and shrug the fabric off of my body. His interest in the coffee immediately shifts to taking in the sight of me in broad daylight.

Brady reaches for me and pulls me to the edge of my bar stool so that I'm between his thighs. "Wow. You should never wear anything, ever."

I say a silent prayer to the Brazillian wax ladies that do such a nice job of keeping me groomed and let myself be pulled even further until he twists me around so that I'm sitting in his lap with my back to his chest. He brings one hand to rest between my legs while the other turns my face to his until he can reach my mouth with his. As our lips collide and our tongues move together, Brady starts to move his other hand in a gentle back and forth motion until I can feel just how wet I am on his fingers.

The kiss becomes more urgent as he continues to tease me. I push backwards so that I can repay the favor; my ass driving right up against his erect cock.

"Damn, Paige."

Once again, I find myself in that place where I'm all sensation and unable to vocalize. I let my actions tell the story; my body lets him know that I want him.

I want him right now.

He takes the hint and stands us both up, bending me over the bar stool and caressing my ass with both hands. After a moment, he pulls back a bit until I feel him start to rub his cock against my throbbing clit. I arch my back as sounds that I barely recognize fight their way out of my throat.

He halts his movement and I whimper. "Sorry, Paige. Just one second."

I've never seen someone move so fast. He streaks across the hallway into my office and is back again in seconds. I hear the tell tale crinkle of a condom wrapper being torn into and I'm relieved that I never even had to ask. He just knew to be safe.

Brady moves back behind me to resume where we left off, but when he doesn't touch me again after a minute or two, I start to get antsy.

"Brady?"

"God, Paige, how did this happen?"

I freeze. He sounds horrified and I don't have to turn around to know what he is talking about. In all the talk about being free and walking around naked, I completely forgot about my scar. It is six inches long, jagged, and an angry red. It barely faded over the years; it was too deep and not tended to until many hours after the wound was caused.

And the scar runs from my inner thigh, right beside my center, all the way to the underside of my ass.

It *is* horrifying. I never realized it before, but anytime in the past that I've been in a position to be undressed with a guy, the lights have always been off.

I dash over and pick my robe up off of the floor and wrap it back around me.

In a shaky voice, I manage to give a vague response. "It was an accident."

Lie.

He knows. "That doesn't look like an accident."

His face is drawn into hard, angry lines. I've never seen him like this before; he is almost always easygoing and playful. I'm not the type of girl that can be under one's scrutiny for too long before I lash out. Because I've had enough drama to last me a lifetime, I need to remove myself from the situation before I say something I'll regret. And by this point, I'm fairly certain that Brady can see right through my bitch routine.

"I think you're right about calling Victor. I won't feel right until I can get this mess cleaned up. Sorry. Would you mind if I went to go and take a shower?"

Brady's smart; he can read the subtext which says I need to be alone for a while. "No, not at all. I could use a shower myself. I'll go back downstairs and clean up, give Victor a call, and then I'll come back up when he gets here. Does that work?"

I give him a grateful smile. "That's perfect."

Neither one of us acknowledges the fact that we both put the brakes on an intensely intimate moment. For now, it's better this way.

FROM YESTERDAY

chapter Twenty-five

I wake up slowly, groggily. My vision takes a while to clear, but when it does I can tell that I am in some old barn. It looks like it has been abandoned for a long time; dust covers almost every surface.

My mouth is covered with a piece of tape and my hands are tied behind my back with rope, but it seems loose somehow and that gives me a sliver of hope. Maybe I could free myself?

I hear someone move and I look to my left.

Nicole.

My sister is bound much in the same way that I am, though her ankles have rope around them while my legs are free. I try to call out to her, but I can't make much sound through the tape. We lock eyes, though, and I'm not surprised to find anger in her eyes rather than fear. Actually, her expression has more of a murderous rage to it. That could prove to be useful.

"Oh, good. You two are finally awake. I was getting bored."

Turner struts into the barn wielding a hunting knife with a serrated edge. He twirls it in his hand and makes it look even more menacing than it otherwise would. I don't like knives.

"How do you like your accommodations, ladies? Isn't this place great? It used to be my family farm, before the economy took a nosedive and we lost it. Now it just sits here as property of the bank. Completely uninhabited. Acres of land. Where no one will hear you scream."

He laughs as if he's told a hilarious joke and I start to really feel the impact of the situation we are in. I didn't let myself believe it before, but now I really do think we are going to die. This lunatic is going to carve me and Nicole up with that knife and bury us where no one will ever find us.

Turner comes closer to the old bale of hay that we are leaned up against. I am beginning to tremble, but I don't want to give him the satisfaction of seeing just how scared I am. He stops in front of Nicole first. I notice a gun tucked in the back of his pants when he leans down to face her. Will he shoot us or stab us? Either option would be effective.

"It wasn't supposed to happen this way, Nicole. You and I were going to enjoy one another's company for a while longer. You shouldn't have brought your little sister over tonight. She could be safe at home with your parents tonight. Selfish bitch that you are, you got her into this mess."

Nicole's rage intensifies with the hate she feels for him. I can tell by the deadpan look in her eyes, the crinkle between her brows, and the pursing of her lips even through the duct tape. Turner has the hunting knife by the blade and he holds it up in front of her, taunting her. She doesn't even flinch.

FROM YESTERDAY

Her lack of reaction seems to throw Turner off his game because he halts hi little intimidation game right in the middle of it and comes over to me.

"You know, Rebecca, you really are a cute girl. Almost prettier than your sister, even though you two have such similar features. I'll bet in a few years, if you get to live past the age of fourteen, you'll surpass her beauty by far. It may have to do with personality more than physical looks. Your sister is kind of a bitch."

He turns the knife over with both hands so that he grasps it by the handle. He lowers it to my face, dragging the tip lightly down my cheek. He doesn't cut into my flesh; at least not yet. He continues the path down to the top of my sweater and pauses.

"So, pretty girl, how would you like to take your big sisters place?"

He rips the top of my sweater open with the knife and I hear Nicole trying to scream through her gag. Turner continues to tear at the rest of my top until my bra is exposed. I wriggle around, disgusted as much as terrified, and then my wrist restraint gets caught on something.

Turner leaves my bra in place, but now he sets his knife down and starts to pull off my leggings. This must have been his plan all along; there's no other reason why he would tie Nicole's ankles and not mine. He is going to rape me and make my sister watch. I cannot let that happen. I try pulling back on the rope around the hands as he busies himself with undressing me, but I can't get them loose enough by the time he has the pants off and takes that damn knife to my panties.

No.

I do the only thing I can think of and kick one leg out as hard as I can. Because Turner knelt down so low, he has provided me with an easy target and I connect with his groin. Hard.

"Fucking bitch," *he swears.*

He grabs himself and sways a little. I work frantically at the rope; it's almost loose enough to slip free. I am grateful that Turner is so obviously terrible at tying knots.

Unfortunately, he recovers far quicker than I had anticipated and in an instant he's got his knife in hand and straddles me.

"Not going to be so nice this time, you hear me?"

I try to raise my leg again, but he is too fast for me. He grabs me by the thigh and forces my knees open wider.

"You won't do that again. And since you ruined a perfectly good erection, I think I'll fuck you with my knife instead."

The pain of the knife ripping through my skin is immediate and overwhelming. He cuts into the underside of my thigh and drags the serrated edge up, until the pain spreads very near my most sensitive area and I'm about to beg him to kill me instead.

My perception of time falters with the agony and I don't know how long goes by, but it feels like an eternity before I can focus on why the cutting stopped.

Nicole stands over Turner and holds his gun in her hands. I know it's the one I saw because he's facing her now, not me, and the back of his pants no longer holds it. I don't know how she managed to get out of her restraints, but I have never been so grateful for her before. Which says a lot for a sister I adore.

She steadies the gun in one hand and uses the other to peel the duct tape from her mouth. It must hurt, but she doesn't seem to care.

"Back away from her, Turner. Now, or I'll kill you this very second."

He starts to step away from both us, but at the last second he changes his mind and lunges for my sister. They both hit the ground and I hear the gun clatter away from them and a but closer to me. Turner and Nicole struggle to get ahead of the other and grab the gun but they forget about one thing.

Me.

I have harnessed all that pain from my wounded leg to finally wrench my hands through the crappy rope and I reach the gun before either one of them. The problem is, I don't know how to use it.

I rip the duct tape off of my own mouth and the sting is nothing compared to my other wound.

"Stop!" I yell.

They stop. Nicole gets up first and comes towards me with her hand held out.

"I'll do it, Rebecca. It's my responsibility. Give me the gun, please."

I want to, but I can't let go of it. I'm shaking and I can't look at anything other than Turner, who has also gotten off the ground.

Nicole glances back at him and sees him, too.

She turns back to me. "Rebecca, give me the gun."

She's pleading with me, but I'm so confused. I don't want Turner to cut me again. I don't want him to touch me.

Too late.

Turner is upon us and I panic. I squeeze the trigger and the gun goes off.

Chapter Twenty-six

I take a super long shower and turn the water as hot as I can. It can't erase those memories, but the sting of the water on my stitched up arm actually has a cathartic effect. Only after the water starts to run lukewarm do I get out. I thought that I had made peace with that scar on my thigh, so it bothers me that I reacted so badly when Brady saw it.

Yes, it's true that I've only had sex in the dark before, but the possibility was always there that someone would see it.

Of course, none of those guys were anything more than an opportunity for me to prove that I wasn't damaged goods. One night stands; both of them.

I dry my hair so that it doesn't get frizzy and then put it up in a twist. Sweats and a t-shirt are as much as I feel like wearing today in the solemn mood I'm in.

I check my cell phone and see a new text from Brady.

Victor is working at the front desk until three. He will come up to your place right after. Do you want me there as well?

I sigh. I feel as though Brady wouldn't have even bothered asking if I wanted him here before I practically kicked him out earlier. I didn't mean to and I really regret it. I wish I could start this day over. I can't, but I do have an hour to fix one thing before this guy comes and plays detective in my very private life.

I don't want you to come over when Victor does. I want you to come over now. I'm a pain in the ass and I don't deserve you, but come over anyway?

I hesitate for a moment before I hit the send button. Did I really just call myself a pain in the ass? Yes, because it is the truth and because it will lighten the mood a little bit. It can be tiring being so damn intense all the time, and I'm used to me. What it must be like to be the person dealing with me, I have no idea. Definitely not easy.

I hit send and wait for his reply.

And continue to wait.

After about 15 minutes, I throw the phone on the floor of my bedroom and lay down on my bed to feel sorry for myself. Sorry for screwing up what could have been the only emotional connection I've ever managed with a guy. I draw my knees up and wring my hands together in frustration.

"You left the door unlocked, Paige."

"Agh!"

I flip over on the bed and fall out of it, landing roughly on the floor.

Brady laughs hysterically.

"You scared the life out of me. Couldn't you have made some noise or something?"

He holds his hand out and when I grab it, he pulls me up to a standing position with almost no effort. I'm kind of impressed.

"I wanted to teach you a lesson in leaving the door unlocked, seeing as you are being stalked by a psycho, so I crept in quietly."

His voice raises several octaves when he mentions my being stalked by a crazy person. It would actually be quite comical, if it were not really true.

"You're right. I wasn't being careful and I should be. I'm happy you came over, though. I didn't think you were going to."

Brady grins. "I figured that responding to your text would be redundant if I was just going to show up anyway. And it was a good move on my part because seeing you fall out of your bed was priceless."

"Thanks a lot!"

I grab one of my pillows off of the bed and swat him with it. He gets this mischievous glint in his eyes and smiles widely.

"Oh, Paige. You are in for it now."

I back away from Brady slowly and giggle nervously as

he advances on me like a tiger ready to pounce. I try to fake him out by pretending to run for the en suite bathroom and then darting around him for the hallway instead, but he's too fast and he catches me. He lifts me off of my feet and then tosses me onto my bed, but he doesn't let go.

"Are you ticklish, Paige?"

Without waiting for a reply, he climbs up on the bed, gets on his knees, and then holds himself over me as he starts to tickle my sides. The answer to his question would have been very much a yes; now I'm laughing uncontrollably and squirming to no avail.

"No. Ugh. More. Please."

It's the best I can manage to get out in between the laughter. As nice as it is to see that I haven't messed everything up and we are still friends after the earlier debacle, it would really suck if he tickled me so hard that I peed on myself in front of him.

Mercifully, he stops the tickle torture and rolls over onto his back. We lay still for a moment, listening to one another breathe.

Brady turns on to his side and lifts up on one elbow to face me. "Hey."

I look back at him, nearly losing myself in those light blue eyes. "Hey yourself."

He leans over to kiss me on the mouth. Soft and quick

with no tongue, but there is still meaning behind that kiss.

"I didn't ruin everything, did I?"

Even though I think I know the answer tot hat is no,I ask anyway. I want to hear him say it.

Brady sits up and scoots back to lean against the head board, pulling me with him so that I'm laying against his chest.

"You didn't ruin anything, Paige. I just don't understand how such a confident girl let a little scar get in the way of what would have been really hot sex."

I turn my head to look at him and he winks so I lean against him once more.

"It's pretty awful looking, I'm sure you can agree. I'd actually forgotten about it, which never happens, but did this time. And then you saw it and you sounded horrified. Even immensely confident people have some insecurities. I guess that's one of mine. What if you never want to go anywhere near there again?"

Brady snorts. "Are you serious? I have a penis. I'll *never* not want to go there. I was not criticizing the way you look in any capacity. You're beautiful, Paige. Even your scar is beautiful. What shocked me was the location of it. It upset me because there is no way that you did that by accident. That was done to you, wasn't it?"

I do not answer him. I cannot answer him. Not to tell him

everything now, anyway. My response is to lean back further into his embrace and he gets it. He wraps his arms around me and holds tight.

"You don't have to tell me now. It will just be another thing that we'll hold off on until you're ready. This is still new and we are still building trust between us. Just understand that we are more than just friends and that makes it okay for me to get upset when I see that someone has caused you harm."

"It is annoying how logical you are, you know that?"

Brady tightens his arms around me. "You are an interesting girl. Well, how about this? It would be logical if you were to get undressed right now and band over so that I may inspect that scar of yours very closely and therefore become used to seeing it. Then you won't have to worry anymore."

I laugh. "Not that I'm trying to play modesty here or anything, but as great as that sounds, don't you think we should hold off until after Victor comes up? We don't have *that* much time."

"No, I guess we don't. Thanks for the vote of confidence, though."

Chapter Twenty-Seven

I must have drifted off because Brady's phone rings and I am jerked back to consciousness. I'm still laying back against his chest and the vibrations are soothing as he speaks to the caller.

He hangs up after a moment. "Victor is on his way up, Paige."

I sit up. "Okay, I'm awake."

Brady kneads my shoulders for a minute. It helps relieve some of the tension in them. As we are walking out into the main room, he smacks me on my butt. I give him a sharp look, but then I smile.

"Nice," I say.

He shrugs. "Do you know how many times I have wanted to do that since the day we met?"

There's a knock at the door and I choose to ignore Brady's locker room humor. I find amusement in it too, but there's no need to encourage him. As much as I like him, and I really do, it is almost like we are getting too close rather quickly. That sets off the warning bells in my head that say I am a danger to Brady.

I shake it off and open the door. Victor is one of the few front desk guys that I speak to. He's personable, despite having the look of someone you wouldn't want to meet in a dark alley.

"Please come in."

He steps inside and reaches out to shake my hand. "Hello, Miss Kerimov."

Playfully, I give him the side-eye. "Call me Paige, remember?"

"Sorry, Paige. It is a habit."

Brady comes up behind me. "It took him nearly a month to stop calling me Mr. Quinlan, and we play basketball together on the weekends."

The men do that clap on the upper arm greeting that is what I think of as the male version of a kiss on the cheek between girls.

"Can I get you something to drink, Victor?"

"No, thank you, Miss -- Paige. I would like to see the damage that was done last night."

I lead him to the mess and pause before I get too close. I haven't bothered to put any shoes on today.

Victor takes a cell phone out of his pocket. "Would it be okay with you if I took some pictures?"

I'm starting to feel like I'm in an episode of CSI. "Sure, do whatever you need to. You don't need to ask me. I really appreciate your help and especially your discretion. That is very important to me."

He nods. "Everyone has a right to their privacy as long as they aren't doing anything illegal, I've always believed."

Victor takes some pictures of the floor and then asks me for a plastic sandwich bag or something that he can take part of the broken glass in. I get him one.

He scoops some particles in the bag, making sure they are pieces that have the blood-like substance. "Now, if this is not really blood, and from what I can tell it is fake, then I should be able to use some of my brother's resources to tell me that. If it is blood, then there's not much I can do. I don't have access to a government lab; not to mention that DNA testing would require authorization I don't have and raise many red flags. Plus, it takes weeks, sometimes months to get those results."

Brady, who is wearing athletic shoes, goes to stand next to Victor. "Hey, this is damn nice of you. Paige needs help and she was never going to ask for it so anything that you do is more than we had before. If there is any way to figure out who is messing with her and get them to stop; well, that's the only important thing."

Victor finishes with the broken vase. "Let's get this

cleaned up and talk a bit more about what's been going on, Paige. If you get me a broom, I'll take care of this."

"Oh, no. Please, you're the guest. I'll clean that up."

I get the men settled at the breakfast bar while I go put shoes on and grab a broom and dust pan. It is easy to get the glass off of the hardwood floors, but I have to work harder to get everything out of the carpeting. I'm sure I missed some tiny pieces and won't be able to walk through the living room barefoot for a while.

I toss the bag down the trash chute, and when I walk back inside the apartment, Brady and Victor have already moved into the living room. Victor is on the couch and I sit next to Brady on the love seat.

Victor begins. "I'm going to ask you some questions and some of them may be rather personal, okay? It will help me out if you are as honest as possible."

I brace myself for this. I know he'll ask questions that I can't answer and that bothers me, but I can't talk about that night. I won't.

"Okay, well tell me when this all started."

I tell him what I know. I tell him about the red lipstick. He asks me who Nicole is and I tell him what I told Brady: that she was my sister and she killed herself. Victor isn't stupid; the look in his eyes says he knows there is more to the story than what I am telling him. He asks to see all the other items the stalker has left for me.

While I'm in my bedroom gathering items, I can hear low murmered voices from the other room. Obviously Brady and Victor don't want me to hear their conversation.

Back in the living room, I set everything down on the coffee table and sit back down next to Brady. Immediately, he stands up.

"Paige, I think it would be better if I went back to my place for an hour. You might feel more comfortable talking to Victor without me invading your privacy."

If it was Brady's idea or Victor's, I'm not sure. Either way, I'm grateful. The last thing I was going to do was ask Brady to leave, but with him here I held back too much.

"You're not invading my privacy, Brady. But, that is not a bad idea."

Brady smiles at me, kisses my forehead, and shakes Victor's hand.

"I'll be back soon, Paige. Victor, Saturday at one?"

Victor gives him a thumbs up. "I'll be there. Try to give an old man a break this time. The rest of you guys are all in your twenties."

Brady laughs evilly as he walks out of the apartment.

After he's gone, Victor drops all pretense of going easy on me.

"Here's the thing, Paige. All this, the notes and the lipstick and breaking into your apartment? It's personal. This person knows every detail of whatever happened to you and your sister several years ago. You can be sure of that. Which is why it is almost a certainty that you know this person as well. If you tell me the truth then I may be able to help you figure out who is connected to you or your sister that would be capable of doing this."

So, I tell him. I leave out some things; I don't tell him any of the details of what happened in the barn, but I give him enough of the story so that he will be able to explore any options he thinks may be relevant. I also neglect to mention that I changed my name to get away from my parents, and if that hinders his inquiry in any way, so be it.

"And this Turner guy that was the one who kidnapped you and your sister, is dead?"

"Yes. He died that night. I -- I shot him."

Victor looks morose. "You did what you had to do to save your life and the life of your sister. There is no shame in that. It is unfair that you were put in that position, Paige. That must have been very tough for you to deal with."

I look down at my hands. It's been a long time since I've thought of the way Turner looked t me incredulously as his life bled out from the hole in his chest. "I could have done a better job of dealing with it, believe me."

"I'm sure you did the best you could."

"No, I didn't. And it was worse after Nicole killed herself three months later. Then I had no one. And my parents? They couldn't even look at me. The one person who understood what I was going through went into my parents' home office when she was home alone, stole the key to the gun chest, and shot herself in the head."

A long stretch of silence then. No one can follow that declaration with anything meaningful.

Victor stands up. "I think I have everything that I need for the moment. I've certainly put you through enough. Digging into the past is almost always painful."

I walk him to the door. "Thank you again, Victor. If you need anything else just let me know."

"Paige, you take care of yourself. Get some new locks installed on this door and be extra careful when you are alone."

"I will."

chapter Twenty-eight

After Victor leaves, I take a few moments to collect myself and make sense of all the emotions I have churning up inside my head. It has been a colorful few days. There is the lust that I feel when Brady is around, the fear that someone might want to kill me, and the sorrow that comes with remembering. At least I can add a sense of relief to that list because of Victor and the fact that my vase is no longer spread across the floor.

Throwing myself down on the couch, I grab my phone and scroll through my contacts. It is definitely a limited list; just my parents, Dr. Sullivan, Brady, Elyse, and now Victor. I type a text to Brady letting him know that Victor is gone and he can come back if he wants to, but I erase the message before I send it. He could probably use his space just as much as I can.

I call Elyse instead. I honestly have no idea why. I guess I'm feeling unsettled still and it wouldn't hurt to hear a friendly voice.

"Hi, Paige!"

FROM YESTERDAY

I am always a little surprised by how exuberant she is.

"Hey, Elyse. How's it going?"

"Very well, just making dinner. How are you?"

We chat for a few more minutes about mundane things. She's cooking Garrett's favorite meal, lasagna, because he's leaving on another business trip tomorrow night. I ask her if she's like to fo see a movie or something this weekend, since she'll be all alone. Eventually we run out of things to talk about and we get off of the phone. I resume staring at the ceiling.

When I was a kid, I used to have those glow in the dark star stickers in my room. Malvina found a book with the constellations and we spent two days arranging the stickers as best we could. I think I was nine or ten.

Nicole made fun of us; she thought the star stickers were childish. She had just become a teenager around then so pretty much everything became childish to her. But when a few months had gone by and the stickers stopped glowing at night, it was Nicole who bought me a new package with her saved up allowance money.

Nicole always did things like that. She could ridicule whatever she chose to, but if she loved you then she'd still support the very thing it was she'd laugh at.

I miss her. I hate that the last memory I have of her is a lifeless body with hollow eyes; a hole in her head from which blood and tissue was leaking out.

I shake that image out of my head as I hear someone knock on the door. I get up to answer it and I realize that it is already dark outside. Time must have gotten away from me while I was daydreaming. It has been several hours since Victor left, but I could almost swear it wasn't more than a half an hour ago.

Brady stands in the doorway holding my messenger bag, a pizza box, and a case of beer.

"You left your book bag upstairs yesterday and this is the pizza we never ate. It's cold."

He follows me inside, sets the pizza on the kitchen counter, and puts the beer in the refrigerator.

"Thank you, I didn't even realize my books were not here. What's with the beer?"

He flashes me an impish grin. "It was just sitting in my fridge. I thought it might help you take the edge off and it's never a bad idea to get a hot girl drunk."

"Real nice."

"A for effort? Are you hungry?"

I pull two plates out of the cabinets. "Yes, actually. I just realize that I haven't eaten anything other than coffee today. I'm surprised that I haven't passed out yet."

Brady puts two slices on each plate. "Yeah, coffee doesn't count for having eaten anything."

I nod my head. "Coffee is an essential food group. Look at

the pyramid. I love cold pizza, but I can heat yours up for you."

He points to himself. "College guy. I've eaten a cold pizza once or twice."

"Good point. Do you want eat this here or over on the couch?"

"Definitely the couch. Ho do you feel about Thursday Night Football?"

I carry our plates towards the living room while Brady grabs two bottles of water and two cans of the beer.

"I love football, especially if the Browns are playing. Is the game on ESPN?"

We set our plates and drinks down on the coffee table and I pass Brady the remote. "No, it's on the NFL Network. Which the association is kind enough to include in the cable package that we pay for with th ridiculous maintenance fees. Want a beer?"

I think about it for a moment. "I don't think I should. I have two classes in the morning."

"It's just a beer. One won't kill you."

I accept the can he is trying to pass me and I take a sip. "Peer pressure? Okay, fine. I'll only have one, though."

"Hey, only drink what you want to. I was kidding about getting you drunk."

I have pizza in my mouth, so it takes me a minute to respond. "I mean, it's not like you would need to get me drunk anyway."

I wink at him.

"Oh, is that so? I'll remember that later, Paige."

The rest of the evening is easy and pleasant in that same manner. We watch the Colts get stomped on by the Patriots, much to Brady's delight. I finish my beer, but I stick to my one drink limit because I'm not a fan of being hung over and stuck in a three hour lecture course. Those classes are tough enough already.

I really enjoy Brady's company and it is great to know that even though the dynamic has been altered from just friendship to something more, we can still sit and hang out like two normal people and there is no weirdness between us. Although, especially after his third beer, I do find it odd that he hasn't asked me to take my clothes off even once since before we started watching the game. Okay, odd isn't the right word because I know he's trying to not overwhelm me. Perhaps it is that I am secretly a bit disappointed.

Which is probably why when the game is over and we've cleaned up from dinner, I take my t-shirt off and throw it at him. My sweat pants I simply shimmy out of and leave laying on the floor of the kitchen in a pool of heather gray material, leaving me in nothing but a pair of dark gray boy shorts.

Brady watches this whole scenario with a surprised, yet

pleased look on his face. My clothing stays where it is; I'd lose the effect if I tried to clean it up after stripping for him, and I start to head down the hall to my bedroom. I can't resist taunting him a bit more, playful mood that I'm in. "Are you waiting for a written invitation?"

He laughs and finally gets himself moving because less than a minute later I feel his hands turning me around to face him. He has my back up against the wall and he places an arm on either side of me, caging me in. I think he'll kiss m or touch me now, but he just looks at me for a few moments. "You're quite the contradiction, aren't you, Paige?"

I play innocent. "What do you mean, Brady?"

"I mean that you're unpredictable. Completely. You keep me at arm's length, and yet you still manage to keep me on the hook. You start to let me in while pushing me even further away. You are very closed off, yet you have more sexual confidence than most of the women your age and it's damn sexy. I cannot figure out who you'll be at any given moment."

I touch my hand to his chest and trail one finger down until I'm hooked onto the waistband of his jeans. "Is this a problem for you, Brady? Do you need to be with someone more stable?"

Looking down, I can literally see the answer to my question as his cock grows erect in his pants.

"No," he says. "Stability is overrated. I'll take moody over boring any day of the week."

And then his mouth is crushing mine and I'm kissing him back fervently. He cups one of my breasts and teases the nipple simultaneously. I make an involuntary noise from the back of my throat. "Oh, you like that do you?"

I lean forward and press my body against his so that I put pressure right where he needs it most. He closes his eyes for a second and I know I've won. Although I'm not sure what we are competing for.

"Yes," I answer him. "I really like that."

I move from his waistband to where his cock is confined by his jeans and I cup him in my hand. It spurs him into action and before I know it, he has me up off of the floor with my legs wrapped around his waist. My clit is rubbing against his erection and I am this close to shoving my fingers between my legs and getting myself off. Not that I think he'd mind very much. But we've done that already. Tonight I want nothing more than to come with him inside of me.

We are in my bedroom now, but Brady doesn't yet set me down. Instead, he tears his mouth from mine and places some quick kisses at the base of my neck, right at the clavicle. I almost lose myself; my hands come away from the grip I had around his upper body and I'm lucky he has a tight hold on me or else I would have fallen.

This seems ot be his cue to lower me down to the bed. Once I'm out of his grip, he pulls his shirt over his head and tosses it aside. I want his jeans off of him as well, so I unbutton and unzip them before sliding them down his legs.

His boxer briefs are still on, but with his obviously erect cock right at eye level for me, I waste no time in pulling the briefs down a bit and taking him out. My hand circles him at the base and I lean forward to take just a tony taste. His cock jumps. I love that.

Feeling encouraged, this time I take more than a little taste as my mouth encircles the head of his cock and I flick my tongue against the underside, at the seam. Brady immediately pulls my hands from him and pushes me back down on the bed.

"Uh uh, Paige. Do you know how badly I want you? You do that again and I'll completely embarrass myself. Let's get those panties off of you first."

Because I'm laying back, Brady hooks a finger into either side of my boy shorts and slowly starts pulling them off. I am watching and I notice a small damp spot in the fabric at the center. Brady notices as well and touches a finger to my core, feeling for the source of that moisture. "You are so fucking wet. It's incredible."

And then his head is between my legs and I feel him kiss me right above my clit. I squirm. When his tongue is moving against me, I nearly start to convulse.

I'm getting so damn close that I need to stop him now before I lose myself. "Wait, Brady."

He looks up. "Is something wrong?"

"No, I just don't want to come without your cock inside of

me. Please?"

"Like you even have to ask."

It takes him no time to grab a condom from his discarded jeans and roll it on. He settles himself on the bed just over me, placing an arm on either side of me and framing my face with his hands. He begins with a gentle kiss, and soon I feel the tip of his cock teasing me; it drives me crazy and I try raising my hips off of the bed to meet him. Finally, finally, he leans back to a kneeling position, grasps himself with one hand and pulls me more open with the other. He pushes forward and then he's inside me. He keeps his strokes slow at first; long, torturous in and out movements, and then he thrusts into me hard. I make some unintelligible sounds and open my legs wider. Brady grabs one leg and puts it over his shoulder so that he can get deeper inside of me.

I'm so close, yet not right there and after a while longer, his breathing starts to get ragged so I know I don't have much time.

"I don't know how much longer I can hold back, Paige, but I am not coming until you do."

He flips us over so that I'm on top, as he leans against the headboard. I move my hips so that I can feel not just his cock on the inside, but I grind my clit up against his pubic bone and create extra friction. It's almost enough and then Brady dips his hand in between us and we both watch as two of his fingers find my clit and rub.

FROM YESTERDAY

That does it. I'm orgasming for what seems like an eternity, my moans so loud I drown my thoughts right out. Not that I can think in this moment.

"Fuck."

There's something so sexy about that desperate cursing when a man starts to come. Perhaps it is the only time those words are appropriate. I ride out the last of my muscle spasms as Brady violently bucks beneath me.

Exhausted, I lay back away from him with even as his cock still twitches inside me. Only the sounds of heavy breathing can be heard now.

When we're both recovered enough, Brady get up, repositions me so that my head is on the pillows and goes to dispose of the condom.

I'm half asleep when he comes back from using the bathroom, washing his hands, and brushing his teeth, but I get up anyway so that I can do the same. Not nearly as comfortable as he is, I shut the door while I pee. I wash my hands and brush my teeth, too. When I get back to my bed I hear the heavy breathing of someone who is obviously asleep and I have to really work hard to get myself under my blanket because Brady is passed out on top of the covers. I shove him in the side gently, sort of, and he wakes up just enough to pull the blanket over both of us, turn me towards him, and the he's asleep again with his hands cupping my ass.

Chapter Twenty-nine

I wake up in the middle of the night dying of thirst, so I get up and wander into the kitchen for some water. I don't bother with my robe this time. I set the ice maker to crushed and fill my glass with little shards of ice and lots of water. After I drink the entire glass, I lean against the counter and start chewing the crushed ice. I've always loved doing that. I just kind of drift around in my head for a few minutes, enjoying the feeling of being just fucked and sore.

Brady comes strolling into the kitchen at some point later, though I'm not sure how much later, looking sleepy and disoriented. Not so much that he doesn't notice me focusing my gaze on his cock which, while not currently erect, is still a nice thing to look at as it hits heavily against his thigh with every step.

He smirks at me. "I like a woman who will check me out and not be shy about it."

"I don't feel like I should be bashful about wanting to look at you naked. You do naked well."

Brady raises an eyebrow. "Oh, yeah? You should see how well *you* do naked. No comparison."

I chew on some more ice. "It's not like I'm going to argue with you."

He laughs. "Isn't chewing on ice cubes supposed to indicate a sign of sexual frustration?"

"Well, I just had sex and I had a fucking great orgasm so I'm going to have to go ahead and say that, no, chewing ice is not frustration. More than likely, it is probably closer to a sign that I have an oral fixation."

There. Let him mull that one over in his head for a while. And he does because the sleep starts to clear from his head and I notice his cock start to thicken.

"For such a beautiful girl, Paige, you're actually sort of evil, you know?"

I smile one of those secret smiles that makes people think you're up to something.

Brady holds his arms open. "Come here. I want to show you something."

I make my way around the counter slowly; doing my best to draw it out and make him wait. When I finally get within Brady's reach, he hoists me up off of the ground and throws me over his shoulder with my ass in the air.

I yelp from surprise.

Brady smacks my butt lightly. "Now this view I definitely

love."

In retaliation, I slap one side of his ass a lot harder than he did to me.

"Now you're in for it, Paige."

He practically runs with me back into my bedroom, but he has to stop in the doorway because it is pitch black in here and neither of us can see a thing.

"Swing around," I tell him. "I should be able to find the light switch."

I do locate the switch and the room is bathed in light too harsh for either of us since the only light we'd used in the kitchen was whatever city lights filtered in through the sliding glass doors.

When I can finally open my eyes more than just a slit, I see the wrong color on the floor. The carpet in my bedroom is beige.

"Son of a bitch."

Brady notices the big red splotches at the same time that I do. It is red all over the far side of my room; most of it concentrated in front of the glass doors that lead to the smaller balcony. It looks like someone bled to death over there, as I'm sure it was intended to. I can tell it isn't actually blood, though. I didn't notice at first, though now I recall something smelling off when I got up for the water, but the room smells strongly of paint.

FROM YESTERDAY

"Brady."

I clutch at my chest; I think this is probably the worst thing the psycho has done.

Because the only time that the red paint could have been poured out like that was when Brady and I were asleep in my bed.

Chapter Thirty

Brady starts moving round the room, gathering up whatever clothing of his he can find.

"Throw something on, Paige. We're spending the rest of the night at my place."

In my closet, the first thing I see is a black and white striped racer back dress that comes to my ankles. I throw it on, not caring that it is way too formal just to go down three flights of stairs. Black flip flop sandals and I'm all set.

Brady comes back into my bedroom with my gun. "Did you know you left this out on your desk?"

"I guess I got too caught up in-- well, us. I completely forgot. I haven't left the apartment since, though."

Brady scrubs his hand over his face in frustration. "That's not the point, Paige. Obviously being inside your apartment isn't helping. Whoever this is has access to your place. They could have taken your gun, again, and shot you."

I cringe. Brady thinks it's because he's scared me with the

all the possibilities he lays out, but actually I'm never comfortable with the idea of shooting someone. That gun is only ever to be used in an extreme life or death situation.

"Yes, Paige. Now you see. These safety measures have to be taken seriously. And you need to get those locks changed. Promise me you'll do that as soon as we wake up?"

"I promise."

"Thank you." He gestures to the gun in his hand. "We'll take this with us. If there's anything you need for the morning, grab it quickly. I want to get you out of here."

I get some toiletries out of my bathroom and toss them into my purse. When I finish, Brady gives me my gun to put in my bag. I have a special holster that's stitched into this bag. Glocks don't have traditional safeties; the trigger is the safety so it has to be stored properly to avoid an accidental discharge. Purses with holsters are the most common way for a woman to carry a concealed weapon because we tend to wear clothing that is form fitting and there is no place on the body to hide a gun.

I make sure to lock my apartment when we leave. The ride in the elevator is quick and then we're in Brady's place and I feel better instantly.

Brady leads me through the hallway to his bedroom with his hand on the small of my back and I'm not sure who's more comforted by that. We are both pretty freaked out. He doesn't say it, but I can tell by how upset he was with me about the gun and how uncharacteristically quiet he is being now. In fact, he says nothing until we enter his bedroom and I stop walking and stare at him.

"I shouldn't have yelled at you," he says when I cross my arms over my chest, challenging him.

I drop my arms to my sides. "No, but I know you just did it because I'm careless sometimes."

Brady looks up and his face scrunches up in confusion. "It just doesn't make sense, though, if you think about it."

"What do you mean? What doesn't make sense?"

He looks back at me, but I feel like he's looking through me as his thought process works his mind out. "The things that happen. It's like this person just wants you to know that they've been there, but nothing else really happens. Sure, there have been some threatening advances, and the things being done are creepy, but it never escalates. Don't these stalker types try to physically harm their prey? What kind of game are they playing?"

I sit down on his bed and my hands fidget in my lap. "I don't know. I've thought about this, too. Maybe that's why I've been less diligent than I should have been. It's like, the only thing they've been trying to accomplish is to remind me of that night. To make me feel guilty. Maybe even to keep me from getting over everything that happened with my sister and her death."

Too late, I realize I've said more than I should.

FROM YESTERDAY

"What do you mean about 'what happened that night'?"

I shift on the bed to look in his direction. "It's nothing. It is all in the past, I'm just rambling. Are you coming to bed? I'm tired."

"Well, I would, but there's a rule I have about that bed."

I relax as his normal flirtations seem to be coming back. "Oh? And what is this rule?"

Brady takes his shirt off. "No clothing allowed. If you want to sleep in my bed, you'll do so completely nude."

I grin as he continues undressing. "So I guess I'll sleep on the couch then."

I stand up and pretend to walk towards the hallway, but I don't make it two steps before a hand snakes around my waist and pulls me back. "Not a chance, Paige. Way to think of a loophole, though. Well played."

I turn to face him and in one swift move, I pull my dress over my head and drop it at his feet. He traces my lips with his right index finger., then trails it down my chin to my chest and stops just above my breasts. "We really should get some sleep," he says.

"Yes," I agree. "There is plenty of time for this tomorrow. After class."

Brady groans as he finishes stripping. "You're still going to class? We've had less than two hours of sleep and it is four thirty in the morning. At best, we'll get two more hours of sleep. I think we might be entitled to skip this class on account of extenuating circumstances."

I slip into the bed and get under the comforter. "When did you become pre-law? Good argument, but you are welcome to do what you wish. I just don't want to miss class unless I'm really sick or something. Reyes takes attendance, remember?"

He gets in bed behind me and pulls me to his chest. "You're right. I'll go. I guess I'm just a little cranky when sleep-deprived. Plus, I used up a lot of energy earlier."

I laugh. "I'd say we both did. Don't worry, we'll be fine. Think of this as a two hour power nap."

FROM YESTERDAY

Chapter Thirty-one

Because Brady only had one class to my two, I have to convince him to let me find my own way back to his apartment when school is done for the day. He tried to insist on coming to my second class with me, but I flat out refused. The only thing that he agreed to was me taking my car instead of walking.

I knock on Brady's door with my overnight bag in hand. He's going to be mad that I went up to my place alone, but after having to wear the striped maxi dress to class today, I wanted a choice of clothing with me. The dress is fairly see through, which Brady so kindly pointed out.

Brady opens the door right away and his eyes fall right to the bag with my clothes. Surprisingly, he says nothing; just steps out of the way to let me in and shuts the door behind me. He takes the bag from me and carries it to the bedroom while I stand awkwardly in the foyer.

He comes back out and sees me standing there. "What are you doing?"

I shrug. "I don't know. I guess I was waiting for you to come back."

"Uh, why? Make yourself at home."

I look around for a second. "I guess it's just habit. My parents taught me to never act inappropriately in someone else's home."

"You slept in my bed with me last night. Naked. I'd say we're past that. Relax."

"Fine." I use a bar stool for leverage to get myself up on the kitchen counter and sit with my legs up on the top of the same stool, parted slightly. The length of the dress keeps it from being obscene, which is good because I'm still not wearing panties. Brady has the same galley kitchen with the island/counter/breakfast bar and three high top stools just like all the other units in this building that I've seen. The surface I'm sitting on is about six feet long and three feet wide. I wonder how it feel to have him come over here and fuck me up against this counter.

Perhaps I'm a bit overloaded on the hormones right now.

"Very nice, Paige. Keep testing me. See what happens."

I part my legs even more. "Uh huh. Speaking of which, I can't believe you didn't say anything about me going upstairs alone to get my stuff."

He throws his hands in the air. "What can I do? It's not like you are very good at taking advice that could keep you safe. I wasn't surprised."

He comes over to sit at the breakfast bar, holding my legs up and then resting them in his lap after he sits in the same stool I was using. "How was your second class?"

I sigh. "More boring than usual. Oh, I called the locksmith on my way back and they are sending someone tonight between four and eight."

"That's great. Did you also call Victor?"

"I did. He actually met me upstairs earlier when I got my things. So I wasn't alone." I smirk at Brady. "He said that the red crap on my vase was not blood. His brother has a friend that is a Chemistry professor at the community college. I guess that school just spent several million dollar on a brand new science complex and they some machine with a name I cannot pronounce. It can read the stuff and spit out all the chemicals used in it. Victor took a sample of the fake blood pool in my bedroom, too."

Brady looks impressed. "That's a great way to start. Did he say when he'd know what the stuff is?"

I shake my head. "No, he's not sure when the professor will have time to help him out. That guy is the only one with access to the machine and he does all the testing for the department so it might be a few days before he can get to us."

Brady looks at his watch. "Well, it is only one. We have at least three hours to kill until the locksmith. What would you like to do?"

To illustrate the point of what *he* would like to do, Brady slips his hand under my dress and slowly drags it upward. I let him get just outside of his goal before I clamp my legs shut with his hand trapped between them.

"Well, actually I talked to Elyse yesterday and she mentioned that Garrett was leaving on a work trip this morning. And I ran into her just now and she looks lonely. So, I may have suggested she come downstairs and hang out with us?"

I say the last part like it's a question when we both know that I've already done what I'm asking and really, Brady can't be mad because we are still just friends, technically, and therefore he's not guaranteed sex whenever he feels like it. At least, I think that's how it works. It isn't as though I have some huge knowledge of how relationships work, or even how to define this one.

Brady does his best to not look disappointed. "No, it's cool. I don't want you to get sick of me anyway, so it's good for you to hang out with your girlfriends. I know she's become important to you."

"Well, I don't want to hang out with just her. I want to spend time with all three of us. But, yes, I guess she has kind of become someone I care about. I don't even know when that happened. She's just got such a kindness about her. Not too many people like that, you know."

"That's true. Are you hungry? I can see what I have. Is Elyse coming down now? Maybe I should order food."

Before I can answer him, there is a knock at the door, which must be Elyse.

Brady stands up and then gives me a hand to help me down from the counter. "Well, I guess that answers one question."

Elyse answers the other question as she is loaded up with at least five different kinds of sandwiches and one of those edible fruit arrangements. I love those, especially if they also have the chocolate covered marshmallows. And this one does.

"I feel like you're always feeding me, Elyse."

She smiles. "It's fun for me, Paige. Maybe one day I'll open up a restaurant."

Elyse arranges the food and points out the sandwich fillings. I take the one with grilled vegetables, Elyse takes the roasted chicken, and Brady takes a roast beef and a tuna salad sandwich. We bring everything over to the gigantic television and start playing a movie that Elyse brought. It's an older movie, but Mike Myers is great, especially when he also plays his character's father with a Scottish accent.

Brady falls asleep at some point during the movie. When it is over, Elyse and I carry the dishes back to the kitchen and repeat the other night by cleaning up together.

We are talking a little bit about Garrett's work schedule and how much Elyse hates it when she confides in me that she suspects he might be seeing someone on the side.

"I mean, I don't want to believe it, but he's been so distracted since we moved here. He's changed a lot in the past few months. And the constant work trips? They were supposed to stop sending him all around."

I am not sure what to tell her. "Well, what specifically has you worried that he is cheating? Did you find something?"

She shakes her head. "No, actually. There's nothing physical to suggest that he is with another woman. It's just this nagging feeling. I just really pray that I'm wrong."

"Maybe his job is really the thing you are jealous of. What is that he does?"

"He is the head of the consumer relations department for a computer supply company. They are pretty big distributors of computer and office supplies for a lot of businesses in the Midwest. They are expanding the company, which is how we ended up here"

When I am quiet for a few moments too many, Elyse changes the subject. "So, Paige. It looks like things are really progressing with you and Brady, yes?"

I glance over to make sure he's still sleeping. He is. "If you're asking if we're having sex, then yes."

Amusement comes over Elyse's expression. "Straight to the point. I love that. So, is it a casual thing or are you a couple?"

"Well, we are friends. There's nothing casual about it for

me, but I haven't asked him about that. And we just stared sleeping together, like, yesterday. I really like him and there's no one else I want. Does that answer your question?"

She touches my shoulder. "I hope it works out for the two of you. I really think you two are a good match."

We finish cleaning up and Elyse excuses herself to go back home and do whatever it is she does. Once she's gone, I decide Brady has slept for long enough and I go over to where he's napping on the couch and I gently straddle his hips, lowering myself forward so that I'm able to touch his lips with my own. He must wake up immediately because his strong hands go to my hips and hold me in place so that I can feel his rapidly forming erection.

"Do you always wake up hard?" I ask.

"Most of the time, but definitely when you sit on my cock and act like my personal alarm clock."

I rotate my hips once or twice and elicit a groan from him. "Okay. Noted. It is 3:45 so I need to go up and wait for the locksmith."

"Oh, man. You're killing me. Okay, give me a minute and then I'll come up with you."

I get off of his lap. "Interesting choice of words."

He gets up and holds my head in his hands. We kiss; a slow, deep, hungry kiss that leaves me practically breathless. And as he heads off towards his bedroom he says, "For the record, it's not casual for me either. I don't want any other girls, just you. You can call us just friends all you want to, but you and I both know that this is something real. The sooner you stop denying it, you'll feel much better about the fact that you're all mine."

"You were faking!" I take the hair clip out of my hair and throw it at his retreating form, beaming him in the back of the head.

"You should play baseball," he calls back. "Maybe then you'll stop throwing things at me."

Chapter Thirty-Two

The locksmith gets to my place by six and I'm thrilled that I don't have to wait any longer because I am impatient tonight. Brady and I have been sitting around playing grab ass for the last two hours without any results because no one wants to get in too deep only to have the locksmith arrive mid-coitus.

The guy spends about half an hour drilling things in the door and changing stuff out. He shows me how the new lock system works and I'm glad Brady is paying attention because the inner working mechanisms of the door handle bores me to tears. By the time the guy leaves, I'm ready to tear off my clothes and throw myself at Brady.

I doubt he would mind.

After I try out the new set of keys and verify that they work, I turn to Brady and put my hands on my hips.

"You look like you're waiting for something, Paige. How can I help you?"

"Are you kidding me?"

He laughs.

I pout. "Okay, you are kidding. Because I know you're just as turned on as I am."

He comes over to me and kisses my neck. "You know I am. I just really enjoyed hearing you say that."

The discussion ends there as his mouth comes down on mine. The kisses are more frenzied than ever; neither of us have any pretense of control.

We get our clothes off in between kisses and try to make it out of the living room, but we are barely in the hallway before Brady pushes me up against the wall, puts my hand on his cock, and returns the favor by rubbing me between my legs. I grip him as hard as I can manage without causing pain and stroke him. He moans into my mouth and I know exactly how he feels because I'm spinning out of it myself.

The tip of his cock produces a small amount of fluid and I rub my thumb over it to use as lubrication as I continue pumping his shaft. I like the foreplay, I really do, but right now I just want him to thrust inside of me and make me forget who I am.

Brady can read minds. Or at least, great minds think alike because the second that those thoughts pop into my head, he turns me around to face the wall and enters me swiftly. The initial thrust makes me wince, but only in extreme pleasure. No pain.

FROM YESTERDAY

He brings one hand around me to rub my clit while he fucks me from behind. When he pauses and pulls out of me, I cry out in despair. He whispers in my ear, his breath tickling my neck. "Wait just one second, gorgeous."

He's back quickly, tearing into the condom packet he brings with him and I remain facing the wall while I wait for him to put the condom on.

Finally, he's back behind me, the tip of his cock lined up with my core and he plunges back inside of me. A scream rips free from my throat. It's true what they say; sex is a thousand times better when it is with someone you care about and cares for you. Otherwise it feels empty afterward. I have the impression that almost nothing will ever feel better than this.

Brady strokes my clit furiously as he moves inside of me over and over again. It's not long before my knees give out and he is the only thing holding me up.

I start to come and I Brady's name leave my lips before I realize what I'm doing. I spasm around his cock and he increases his pace.

"Fuck, Paige."

The word for the sounds he makes now is grunting, which sounds as far from sexy as possible; but to hear im actually making the noise is so hot. I would never get tired of hearing him come.

And then we're both sweaty and breathing hard. Brady uses the last bit of strength to lift me up and get us both to my bed. We fall asleep in a tangle of limbs.

I wake up a few hours later; hot from all the body heat. I do my best not wake Brady up as I extricate myself from his hold on me. I get in the shower and turn the faucet away from the heat so that the water can cool me off. I lather on the coconut-scented body wash and practically drown myself in it. I'm addicted to this scent. I wash my face and then shut off the shower. A big, fluffy towel is waiting for me just outside of the shower door, held up by Brady.

"You should have woken me up, I'd have loved to soap your back for you."

I try to snatch the towel from him, but he pulls it just out of my reach, puts the towel behind me and wraps it around me himself.

"Sorry," I say, "but you were sleeping so peacefully. I felt guilty waking you."

"In general, it's rare for a man to be annoyed when a beautiful woman wakes him up to take a shower with her. Just for future reference."

"I'll file that way with the rest of the information you've given me. I'm hungry. It's only ten on a Friday night. Would you eat Thai food if I have it delivered?"

"I'll pretty much eat anything. So nothing to worry about there. Do you mind if I grab a quick shower?"

"Not at all. I'll call the order in while you're in here. Pad

FROM YESTERDAY

Thai and Pad Woon Sen with chicken and mushrooms?"

Brady kisses the tip of my nose. "Pad Woon Sen is the dish with clear noodles, right? Perfect. Oh, ask for extra mushrooms, please."

I call for the food and go back to my bedroom to get dressed. Brady is out of the shower already; standing in the room with a towel drying his hair and everything else uncovered. I hang up the towel I was using and go to my closet.

"What do you think you're doing with those clothes?" Brady asks when I emerge with some leggings and a camisole in hand.

"Well, Brady, I don't think I'm going to answer the door for the delivery person wearing nothing. Thank you."

"Fine, use logic against me. If it were up to me, I'd keep you here all to myself and no clothing allowed the whole weekend."

I smile at the thought. "As much fun as that sounds, and it does sound wonderful, eventually we'll ahve to leave my apartment. We aren't even supposed to be in here. We were staying at your place."

Brady puts his boxer briefs on. "Well, the locks have been changed and the circumstances dictated that we stay here for now. We can go back down if you want."

"No, I'm fine here."

The food arrives then and I tip the delivery woman a ridiculous amount for arriving so quickly. She tries to hand the twenty dollar bill back to me, protesting that it's too much, but I wave it away and plead with her to keep it. Apparently, sex makes me ravenous and generous.

Brady and I spend the rest of the night eating and laughing. Once the food coma wears off, we get back in bed and burn off the calories from our dinner. I fall into a sleep so deep that I don't wake up even one time during the night. We set an alarm before going to sleep because Saturday doesn't inspire me to get up very early, but Brady does have plans for basketball in the early afternoon.

Pounding on the door wakes us both up hours before the alarm clock would have gone off. At seven in the morning on a weekend, I'm tempted to just go answer the door completely naked to teach whomever it is a lesson. Thankfully, I throw on a robe first.

Because when I fling the door open, ready to have it out with my early morning wake up call, I come face to face with someone I haven't seen in almost two years.

My father.

Chapter Thirty-Three

I stare at my father; I cannot speak and I cannot move. I have been hiding from my parents for so long that I almost forgot what they looked like. Of course, I can still spot the signs that say he is angry, very angry, yet that does not diminish the fact that I'm his daughter and he loves me. I see that in his eyes, too.

"Papa," I whisper.

He holds his arms out and I waste no time by throwing myself into his embrace and accepting his warmth. I am not even close to forgiving my parents for what they did to me, but that doesn't mean I can't still love them and want them to be there for me.

This happy reunion can't last long, though, and it's over all too soon when my father pulls back and grips my shoulders with enough force to cause a little pain.

"Rebecca, do you have any idea the mess you've made? You check yourself out of the clinic the day you turn eighteen and take off without so much as a goodbye to me or your mother. After everything that happened; after all that we went through with losing your sister, you think that was the right thing to do?"

Stunned into silence both by his presence and the fact that even after all this time he is still blaming me and treating me like a mental patient, I squirm out of his grasp and back up until I am standing in the living room. I spin around and walk over to the sliding glass doors and look out at the incredible view of the city in the early morning light.Behind me, I hear my father shut the door and come over to where I am.

"Rebecca? Did you hear me?"

Staying with my back to him, I finally find my voice. "You threw me in an insane asylum and tossed out the key. Why would I tell you where I was going?"

"Paige? What's going on? Who is this?"

Damn. I forgot all about Brady for a moment. This is not a good situation. I can see the entire life I've built for myself; all the progress I've made in school and finally in personal relationships, it starts to unravel right in front of my eyes.

My father stares at Brady, who is clad only in his underwear. Brady stares back at my father, understanding begins to dawn in his eyes.

"Rebecca," my father's Russian accent gets thicker when he is angry. "You have boyfriend here? In your bed?"

FROM YESTERDAY

Brady looks confused. "Who is Rebecca?"

I don't have a choice now, but to tell the truth. "I'm Rebecca. Paige was Nicole's middle name. When I moved here I used Paige and my mother's maiden name to start over. I left Rebecca Levkin back in that nut house that *you* put me in!"

My finger is pointed towards my father and I can't help but throw one last dig in. "I wasn't crazy. I shouldn't have been there. And even after my doctor told you that I was not delusional, you and Mama kept me in that hospital for over a year."

Brady takes a seat on the couch and puts his head in his hands. "Can someone please explain to me what is going on here?"

"Brady," I say, "maybe my father and I should talk alone for a while."

Of course my father has to twist the knife in a little deeper. "No, Rebecca. The young man deserves an explanation. Let's give him one. Let the boy know exactly what he's getting into." He holds his hand out to Brady. "Dmitri Levkin. Rebecca's father. And you are?"

Brady, still in a bewildered state sitting on my couch in boxer briefs, shakes his hand. "Brady Quinlan. Paige's, uh, undefined relationship friend?"

"So you want to know all about your Paige, Brady?"

Brady crosses his arms over his chest. "I believe I already

know everything I need to know about her. I also know that she went to great length's to get away from you, so I can't imagine you have anything to say that I want to hear. Other than telling us when you're planning on leaving?"

My father nods at Brady; his way of showing respect. "You seem like an upstanding person, Brady. If the circumstances were different, I'm sure I'd like getting to know you. But Rebecca needs help. She needs to come home to her mother and me and see her doctor."

"No! I am not going back. I will never go back there. I'm almost twenty years old, Papa. You have no legal right to take me anywhere and you can't touch my trust fund."

"That's true, Rebecca, but I can have you declared unfit to make decision for yourself. Your mother has her doctor friends."

Brady stands up. "This is out of control. Paige is doing great here. Maybe it's best if you just leave her alone."

My father looks more agitated by the second. "Oh? She is doing great here, yes? So, you're telling me that there have been no 'stalking' incidents?"

My father makes air quotes for emphasis when he says the word stalker.

It was enough to catch Brady's attention. "What do you mean by that?"

"I mean you've fallen into her madness. You see, Rebecca

was a sweet girl that worshiped her older sister. Nicole was her opposite; rebellious, careless, promiscuous. When Rebecca was fourteen and Nicole was seventeen, they went to see an older man that Nicole was spending time with. The man was a disturbed person and he forced the girls to the farm his family had once owned until it fell into disrepair and the bank seized it. He tied them up, but before things went any further, Rebecca was able to get free and she shot the man. He died. Nicole, unable to handle the guilt of having gotten her sister in that situation, took her own life some months later, also with a bullet. It wasn't long before 'incidents' started happening to Rebecca."

Hearing this; this sordid past of mine, come from my father's perspective is much worse than living with the memories. As humans, the only way we can live with ourselves is to justify our own actions inside our heads. If someone else tells your story, it can ruin you. I sink to the floor and brace myself for the rest.

"At first, we thought she was having nightmares, or just forgetting that she'd done something. After some time, though, the things that she claimed were happening got creepier. There was the time that she took one of my guns, a similar model to the one her sister used to end her life, and left it on Rebecca's bed next to a copy of Nicole's suicide note. Rebecca claimed that someone else did that, but she's the only one with access to all these things. She took her sister's favorite lipstick and wrote threatening words on the walls of her own bedroom. Lots of other things like this."

I can't believe what I'm hearing. "After all this time, you still think that I did those things? I told you, it wasn't me! I begged you to help me."

The look on Brady's face is a cross between understanding a missing piece of the puzzle, and fury. The question is, who is he furious at? Me because he believes my father, or my father for not believing in me? I cannot tell.

"We did help you. We love you and we just want you to get better. If you had stayed with that inpatient program, you could have made such progress by now. Instead I find out from a stranger that you're living all the way in Florida and doing these terrible things to yourself again. The only mistake we made was letting that incompetent woman treat you. I should have asked for someone else; someone who would see the truth. That woman encouraged your hallucinations."

I look up sharply. "Wait, what stranger told you this? And, Papa, they were not hallucinations. Even if I had done all that stuff to myself, which I didn't, it still physically happened and you can't say I imagined anything." I look at Brady, pleading with my eyes. "You believe me, Brady. I know you do. You've seen the things that happened."

My father doesn't even give him a chance to answer. "I'm sure you've seen some suspicious looking items appear, and whatnot. Ask yourself this question: is there anything that happened that cannot possibly have been something that Rebecca did herself? At any point, was there another person that you actually saw for yourself doing these pranks?"

He's got Brady on his side now. I can see it. And my father is smart; that is a very convincing argument. It clicks for me now why my stalker never did anything more than leave me notes. This way everything could look like it was happening in my head; that I was doing it to myself. The first time this started happening, back in Ohio, there was a time where I started believing that maybe I was doing this and that I just blocked it out. Dr. Sullivan helped me get past that. She helped me see that I wasn't crazy and I can never thank her enough.

Right now, though? I cannot handle anymore of this. I needed Brady on my side and he is staying way too quiet. This is why you don't yourself care about other people. You always end up getting hurt.

"Both of you can just go to hell," I tell them.

I run out of my apartment barefoot and in my robe. Let those two stay up here and have some Rebecca is crazy bonding session.

Sheer luck is on my side for once, because when I get on the elevator, one of the building's maintenance men is riding down at the same time. They have keys to all the units.

"Oh, thank God! I'm so happy to see you." I give him a winning smile and let the very top of my robe slip open a bit so that my cleavage is on display.

The man grins. "Oh, you are, are you?"

"Absolutely. I locked myself out of my apartment and, well, as you can see, I'm not exactly dressed for the outside world. If you help me, it will save me from having to walk through the lobby like this."

He looks down my robe. "Well, you look good to me. But I'd be happy to help. What unit?"

The elevator car stops on the twenty-second floor. "Unit 2205."

We get out and I wait while he fumbles with his set of keys. I feel disgusted with myself for practically bearing the tops of my breasts to this lecherous middle-aged man, but desperate times and all that. He opens the door to Brady's apartment.

"Thank you," I say. "You have no idea how much I appreciate this."

His mouth turns up in a greasy smile that makes my stomach turn. "Well, what about I come in and you show me how much you appreciate this?"

"Over my cold, dead body."

I slam the door in his face and throw the deadbolt. He pounds on the door twice, then I hear him yell that I'm a bitch and he's gone.

I look around Brady's place in a panic. What do I do? I need a plan. I take a few deep breaths and I start to clear my head so that I can think.

FROM YESTERDAY

I go into the bedroom and grab my overnight bag. I am thrilled that I left it down here last night. There are clothes in here, and my purse with my wallet and cell phone. I get dressed, grab my keys, and then duck back out into the hall. I check for the maintenance man or my father and Brady. No one is around so I'm good to go. I take the stairs down to the third floor parking garage and make a beeline for my car. I can go anywhere I want. I will come up with a new name that has nothing to do with my sister or my mother. I will *not* make any friends. I won't even go to school, which is a tough pill to swallow because when most little girls are dreaming fo their wedding, I have dreamed of walking across the stage at my college graduation. Maybe later in life.

I'm on the road for half an hour, all the way in Boca, when Elyse calls. It isn't the first phone call I've had; both Brady and my father have been trying me over and over again, but it's the only one I will answer. I'm not sure why, but maybe I just want to say goodbye to the one true friend I've made.

"Elyse?"

"I knew he was hiding something from me, but I thought he was cheating. When I went to look through his desk I found the key to his filing cabinet. Oh, God, Paige."

She crying hard and it isn't easy to understand what she's saying. I see an exit coming up and I get in that lane so I can get off of I-95. "What did you find, Elyse? What was in the cabinet."

I slow down as I make my way down the off-ramp and pull into the parking lot of an empty high school.

"There were documents about two girls; young ones. Newspaper clippings about those girls and his brother. I didn't even know he'd had a brother! The brother is dead. None of it made sense until I found the pictures."

It is a damn good thing that I pulled my car over because I begin to feel lightheaded. Puzzle pieces start to click together. The red dye on my vase and all over my floor.

'What does Garrett do?'

'He is the head of the consumer relations department for a computer supply company. They are pretty big distributors of computer and office supplies.'

"Elyse, what did you see in the pictures you found?"

"Pictures of you, Paige. From years ago and from now. Like he'd been spying on you. Pictures of a girl that looks like you. Pictures taken of you and Brady. And weird stuff, like lipstick on a mirror."

My heart stops. "Where is he right now, Elyse?"

"He flew to Ohio yesterday morning. He's supposed to be back tomorrow."

"Listen to me very carefully, Elyse. You have to get out of there. You can't let him know what you found, okay? Pack a bag and get the hell out of there until I call you. Promise me?"

She cries harder. "Why? What does all of this mean?"

"Just trust me. I will tell you everything when I can. I promise. Just hurry because I have a feeling Garrett isn't in Ohio anymore. I'll call you soon."

"Okay." She hangs up.

I reach inside my purse and feel around until I hit the holster and I pull out my Glock 26. I eject the magazine and pull the slide back. All ten bullets are there. I put the magazine back in and re-holster the gun. And then I turn my car out of the school parking lot, get back on 95, but heading south his time. If I hurry, I can make it back in twenty minutes.

Chapter Thirty-four

There is no one in my apartment when I get back. I check Brady's place and I find the door still unlocked from this morning and no one there either. I call him, but the call goes straight to voice mail several times over. The same thing happens when I try to reach my father.

I call my own voice mail. There are two messages. On of them I only play the first few seconds of because it is my father demanding that I get back here. The second one is the comforting voice of Brady and my eyes tear up when I hear him plead for me to come back because I never gave him a chance to respond. He says he believes me and not my father. So, where is he?

My phone rings again and Elyse's number flashes across the screen but either the call drops or she hangs up after only one ring and it becomes listed as a missed call.

I hope she listened to me and got herself out of here already. I call her back, but I get a busy signal. Something is definitely not right. I go back up to my floor.

FROM YESTERDAY

The door to Elyse's place is cracked open. I put my hand on my gun just in case, but leave it in my purse so that I don't scare her. I tiptoe around the kitchen and bypass the living room. No one.

I see her in the bedroom. She is sitting in a desk chair with her back to me. I rush over to her.

"Elyse! What are you still doing here?"

She doesn't answer and now I see it is because she can't. Her eyes are wide open and so bloodshot that the whites aren't even visible. Bruising around her throat says she's been strangled to death. I touch her neck to check her pulse like they do on television, but the second I touch her ice cold skin I realize there is no point.

Elyse is dead.

And I don't even get a chance to mourn her because my cell phone rings and once again it is Elyse's name on the caller ID.

I pick it up immediately. "Garrett?"

"Yes, how did you know it would be me?"

I take a deep breath. "Because I'm looking at your dead girlfriend right now. Why did you have to kill her? It's me you wanted, not her."

"I came home and found her looking through my private things, Paige. Or can I drop that act and call you Rebecca? She saw things she couldn't know about, Rebecca. Such a genuine woman like that? She would have turned me in."

Every time he says my name, my real name, I hear his brother Turner instead. It makes me sick.

"Turner was your brother?" I ask.

"Yes, he was my younger brother. He wasn't right in the head, and he made some crucial mistakes, but he was family and you and your bitch sister destroyed him. Now I'll take care of you. Come and meet me in the old men's locker room on campus. The one they don't use anymore since they built the new one."

I scoff at him. "Are you kidding? Why would I do that? I don't have a death wish. I think I would prefer to call the police and let them figure you out."

Now it's Garrett who is laughing. "Sure, you can do that, but there are consequences for your actions. Get over here in the next 15 minutes and don't call the cops or I will kill your father and your boyfriend."

He ends the call.

Chapter Thirty-five

The old locker rooms are next to the abandoned stadium on the far side of the campus. It was supposed to have been torn down last year, but there was some kind of delay with the funding of a new project. The place is a complete shambles; the track is worn and cracked, the stadium benches are in pieces, and the grass hasn't been cut in so long that the blades reach past my ankles as I trek through it. I make it to the men's side of the locker rooms within seven minutes of Garrett's phone call.

There is no door, just an entrance that curves around so that no one can see inside the room until they have turned two corners. When the room comes into view, I am struck by such a sense of familiarity that I almost lose my grip on my gun, which is in my right hand at my side.

Brady and my father are bound at the hands at feet, but not with rope. Garrett, obviously smarter than his brother, has secured their limbs with plastic twist ties. There is no slipping through those things, as far as I know. Duct tape around their mouths just like Nicole and I had, though. Brady seems unharmed, but my father has blood running down his forehead from a cut that is possibly up on his scalp because I cannot see the source. They both look at me as I enter the room; identical horrified expressions on their faces. They know what I know: I am probably going to die and tied up like that, there will be nothing that they can do to stop it from happening.

"Stop there, Rebecca. That's far enough,"

Garrett steps out from behind a row of lockers and yanks Brady up to his feet. He puts Brady in front of him like a human shield.

"There, now we can talk without you trying to shoot at me. Wouldn't want to miss me and hit your boyfriend, would you?"

I keep my trigger finger straight; it's never smart to touch the trigger unless you are ready to shoot, but I move it closer so that I can get the gun off faster if I need to.

"I have had a lot of time learning how to properly use guns since I was a kid, Garrett. Because of your brother. I wouldn't be so sure that you're safe just yet."

I hear him click the safety on his gun. It looks like a Sig, and I hope so because the one time I used one it kept jamming on me. It would be great if that would be the case now. Wishful thinking, I suppose. They are supposed to be pretty reliable weapons.

"I'll take my chances."

I am tired of his games. "What are we doing here, Garrett? Tell me what you want from me and I will give it to you. Just let my father and Brady leave."

"Can you give me my brother back?"

"This is just about revenge for you? Nothing to do with money? Because your scum brother let that little secret slip out that night. He told us all about your little kidnapping scheme. How the two of you planned to take Nicole hostage and ask my parents for five million dollars to get her back. Too bad he jumped the gun and ruined your plan. He never mentioned he had a brother, only that he was supposed to wait for someone, but I have figured the rest out today. I knew there was something I didn't like about you when we were at dinner the other night."

Garrett hits Brady in the ribs with the butt of his gun and Brady falters. He wheezes through the tape and goes down to the ground. Hard. Garrett points the gun to his head as I raise my arm and hold my gun out with both hands.

"Watch it. You won't be able to hit me before I put a bullet in his skull. You dumb bitch, you don't know anything. That money was going to change our lives. Our family had that farm in it for at least a hundred years. When the economy took a nose dive we lost everything and it was your father and his business partners that refused to go in with my parents on their plan to develop a new crop that could have saved our farm. After the bank seized the land, my parents had to get minimum wage work that barely paid the rent in our crappy two bedroom apartment. They certainly could no longer afford the medication that Turner needed for his Borderline Personality Disorder. So, I blame you."

He isn't facing me when he talks about placing blame. He has turned to my father.

"No!" I scream, too late.

Garrett shoots my father. It hits him in the chest, on the right side. My father's eye close and he slumps over, blood pouring from his wound.

Garrett turns back to me. "There, that's better. Now as far as the money goes, well, you're going to pick up that pen and piece of paper over there and write down the account number and password to your trust fund. Isn't online banking amazing? I'll verify that this is the correct information, and if it's not, I will shoot Brady in the head. Do it now."

There is little fight left in me. Most of it ran out of the hole in my father's chest. I write down the information.

"Good, now take out that pretty cell phone of yours and login to your account. Unhide the password so that I can see you are typing what you wrote down on that piece of paper."

I do what he asks. When I'm in my account and he's satisfied that I have given him the correct information, he tells me to close the banking app and put the phone away. I have just enough time to hit button in my campus police app before

I get the phone back in my pocket. Now I can only pray that it worked.

"Good job, Rebecca. Now let's address the topic of revenge. Because I already have mine. I took it for my brother, who's life your sister took. Don't look so surprised. My brother had a camera set up in that barn. I saw when you fired that shot and missed. I saw your sister get the gun from you and not miss. I know she was the one who killed him. That's the real reason she shot herself, isn't it?"

I nod. "I have always thought so, yes."

"And I'm sure you already know it was me that started messing with your head back in Ohio. And obviously here. That was for my parents. They started drinking when we lost the farm. My father was drunk the night he lost control of his car and crashed into a tree. My mother died instantly, but he lived for a few hours before they found him. I'm told he suffered horribly until he finally died, pinned in that car. It was a major bonus that you were institutionalized because of the stalking. I didn't intend to make them think it was you, but I ran with it afterward. Good job with the name change, by the way, but next time don't use names associated with your family. It took me a few years, but I found you."

I am surprisingly calm now. I want to keep him talking in the hope that campus police got my signal. "So, was it you that finally went to my father and told him where I was? Why didn't anyone know who you were?"

"It was me. I flew to Cleveland yesterday, went to see him and let him know how to find you. I needed him here so that I could make you suffer more by watching him die. People knew who I was, Rebecca, they just didn't know what I looked like because I was offered a full athletic scholarship to school and was able to remain there even after my parents lost their money. Garrett is my first name, but no one ever used it. Everyone used to call me Tate, because the only thing I would eat as a baby was potato."

My arms are getting tired. I don't know how much longer I can hold the gun at him. The left one is especially sore from using only that when I was giving him my account information.

"Now it's your turn to answer a question, Rebecca. Why did you let everyone believe that you shot Turner and not Nicole?"

I glance at Brady just to make sure he is still breathing. He is, but it looks painful every time he sucks in a breath. He must have a broken rib.

"Nicole was the confident one. She watched out for me. I looked up to her. Our roles were reversed that night. She could not handle having shot your brother, and she did it to save my life. While we waited for the police to get there, I told her. I said, 'just forget what happened. I shot Turner, not you'. I repeated it over and over until I think I had actually convinced her that was what happened. Obviously not, but I tried. She tried to apologize in her suicide note, but only I knew what she meant and I never told anyone."

Brady and I lock eyes. I am losing my grip on the gun and he can see it.

An opportunity presents itself just then. I hear a noise from outside the locker room. Garrett hears it, too.

"What did you do?" he yells. "Did you call the cops, bitch? I'll kill your boyfriend."

When he started yelling at me, Garrett took the gun from Brady's head and pointed it at me. As he goes to move it back, I take my shot. He sees it coming and fires back at me. I miss the kill shot, only hitting him in the shoulder and not even the one he's using to hold his gun.

I drop to the floor. Pain, white hot and searing spreads throughout my abdomen. My vision gets a little cloudy, but I can see Brady trying to move toward me, but Garrett is already standing over me. He puts the gun to my head and I close my eyes and wait to die.

I hear a gunshot.

And I continue to breathe.

I see Garrett hit the floor next to me. Shot in the head, he's gone.

I pass out.

I'm in and out of consciousness while I try and piece time together. I see the campus police and some county officers. Obviously the police app worked. At some point, I'm placed on a stretcher and am taken out of the locker room to an ambulance. I wake up again and feel that ambulance moving and hear the sirens wailing.

An EMT is sitting with me. "You're okay," he says. "The bullet passed right through and was far enough to the side that it didn't hit any major organs."

I try to speak but my voice comes out a whisper. "And the others?"

He smiles. "I know the one guy with the rib injury is okay. Just a fracture. It will heal. The gunshot to the head is gone. And the older man with the chest wound is touch and go. Hey, the pain medication I gave you is kicking in so just relax."

I pass out again.

Chapter Thirty-six

I am next to be called. I'm sitting in my seat, sweating under the heavy graduation gown in the Miami May heat. And then I hear my name.

"Rebecca Levkin."

I jump up and get to the podium where I shake hands with the Dean and take my degree. This is what I've been waiting for my whole life and it's every bit as spectacular as I thought it would be.

After I take my seat again, I look out into the crowd and find my parents. My father spent almost six months in the hospital after he was shot and required several surgeries to repair all the damage surrounding his heart. Initially, he had trouble getting around because his heart could only take so much. He would get tired quickly and it frustrated him. Eventually, he healed up quite nicely and my mother even convinced him to retire.

My parents come down and visit me so often that they

finally caved and bought a condo in nearby Sunny Isles. I tease them about being so Russian that they have to find all their friends, even in a different state. My mother finds it less funny when I refer to the people in their area as comrades. I remind her that she should be happy we have managed to repair our relationship. And we really have. In fact, it's probably better than it ever was. We even call one another one the phone and talk about things I never thought I would discuss with my mother. Like my boyfriend.

Brady sits next to them. He graduated last semester and has already been accepted to Miami University for his Master of Social Work. The school is far, all the way down in Coral Gables and I'm nervous that we won't see much of each other. We'll deal with that as it comes.

Once the ceremony is over, I run to Brady and he lifts me up in the air and spins us around. We kiss, but keep it mild because my parents are watching us.

"Congratulations, Bec!"

It took him a while, but Brady eventually stopped accidentally calling me Paige. Once the secret was out, I wanted to go back to my real name. Rebecca was too long for him, he said, so he started calling me Bec and I'm fine with that. My mother not so much. She gives Brady the side-eye.

He notices. "Sorry, Mrs. Levkin."

"Ignore her," I say. "She loves you."

And it's true. My parents are happy with me and happy

with my choices, including my choice of boyfriend. I have wished for this kind of happiness my entire life. The only thing that dampens the joy I feel is the absence of my sister. Even though I'll never stop missing her, I have finally learned how to cope with her death and stop looking for her in everyone I meet. We honor her every year on her birthday. I also started doing the same for Elyse. We were friends for a short time, but she still made an impact on my life.

"I also love you," I tell him.

He smiles. It took me a long time, way longer than when he said those words to me, but I finally did. How could I not love someone who stuck by me through some of the worst moments of my life, yet managed to make even those times better? He was patient with me while I kept secrets from him. He never even pushed me for the full details of that night; not until he was sure I was ready to tell him

Now I find it easy to love people. I have finally learned the importance of family. I have finally stopped running.

acknowledgements

First and foremost, I have to thank Dr. Michael Hettich. It was his Creative Writing that inspired me to start writing again. Without his encouragement, I would never have decided to do something with my writing. You have my undying gratitude.

Arijana Karcic, who designed my beautiful cover and then basically gave me a self-publishing 101 course. You're truly invaluable.

Bryan Rietter, who gave up his time to make sure this book didn't have too many typos.

Christa Cervone, who let me ask her a million questions about publishing on messenger many nights.

Ana Zaun, who also let me ask her a million questions.

My friends, I wish I could list you all individually, but I cannot. You know who you are. You have supported and encouraged me all along.

My family, these poor people have to put up with a lot!

Thank you to all of these people. Without you, I am nothing.

FROM YESTERDAY

Copyright © 2014 Miriam Epstein

ISBN-13: 978-1497379466

ISBN-10: 1497379466

Made in the USA
Middletown, DE
19 June 2020